For: Fa
"Thanks"
"God Bless"

The Search for Level Ground

Orion Jenkins [signature]

Orion Jenkins

I Love You
Irene [handwritten]

AmErica House
Baltimore

First printing

ISBN: 1-58851-387-4
PUBLISHED BY AMERICA HOUSE BOOK PUBLISHERS
www.publishamerica.com
Baltimore

Printed in the United States of America

For my much-appreciated mother, with love

Ruth Irene Jenkins

Acknowledgements

Thanks to Publish America, Inc. and my editor Kelly Hartman.

Warm thanks to my husband for without his knowledge of computers, this book would never have happened. Special thanks to my best friend, Glenda Brooks, for her encouragement.

Chapter One

My name is Suzanna Stoggins. I live in a small southern town, about thirty miles south of Atlanta, Georgia. I've lived here almost all my life. My story begins in 1952. I was sixteen when my voice came to live within me. The first few times the voice spoke to me, I pushed it aside, telling myself it was my imagination. As time passed, however, the voice didn't go away. I finally realized I would have to talk to someone about the voice. I definitely didn't want to tell my very best friend, for I was afraid she wouldn't be a friend anymore. She might even think I am crazy. I've decided to tell my mother. Mother isn't the most stable person in the world. This is why I haven't talked to her already. I know I can't talk to Daddy, for he is my biggest critic. I can just hear him say, "Suzanna don't get dramatic with me, it's just your wild imagination at work again."

I talked to Mother, and she became hysterical, just as I knew she would. She grabbed the phone, and dialed Doctor Browne's office to make an appointment right away. She told the receptionist that it was an emergency, therefore the receptionist told my mother to bring me in right away. Mother insisted that she should talk to Dr. Browne alone, before I talked to him. I sure wish I were a fly on the wall, to hear what's being said about me. Knowing Mother as well as I do, I'm sure she is falling apart by now. Here she comes, and it's evident that she has been crying. Now it's my turn to see doctor Browne.

"Well now, Suzanna, I've heard your mother's version, how about giving me yours. Tell me all about this voice you hear."

"There's not that much to tell Dr. Browne, I'm aware it's always with me, even when it doesn't speak."

"Uh-huh, tell me Suzanna, has it ever told you to do harm to anyone?"

"Oh no, nothing like that, sometimes it's only a whisper, maybe just to get my attention. It's like someone else is speaking to me from inside me. Sometimes I feel it is there to protect me, then other times it makes me anxious, as if something bad is going to happen."

"And you say this voice has never told you to harm anyone, has it ever suggested that you harm yourself?"

"No, never, I don't feel any evil presence, it's not that kind of voice. Actually I sometimes think its God speaking to me."

Doctor Browne is nodding his head, with a puzzled look on his face. He doesn't seem to have any idea what the voice means, or what to do about it. Then he says he wants to do some blood work. He tells me the tests will be back in a week or so, and his office will call to make another appointment.

On our way home I asked Mother what the doctor told her. I can tell by her mannerism that she is not going to be truthful with me. My mother is an attractive person; she has the most beautiful blue eyes I have ever seen. She has kept her figure all these years. I think Daddy has destroyed all her confidence. Though Daddy is the ruler of our house, and no one, but no one, better challenge him. Mother is from a family of eight, and she is the oldest. Her daddy was a sharecropper in Dothan, Alabama, and it's needless to say they were very poor. Mother told me they only got one pair of shoes a year, and that was in the fall right before it got real cold. My mother's aunt May, married a man from Atlanta, and they both worked at the Fulton Bag Mills. They didn't have any children, so when Aunt May had an operation, and had to have bed rest for six weeks. My grandmother let Mother come to Atlanta to help aunt May, until she could get on her feet again. This is how my mother met my daddy, who lived in Atlanta.

My daddy is an only child, and his daddy owned his own business, therefore my mother thought Daddy's family was rich, and they were compared to Mother's family. Daddy has a college degree, and he runs his own successful business, but he puts himself a notch above my mother. She allows him to tell her what to do, and even what to wear. Daddy is a perfectionist; therefore no one can do anything as well as he can. I have never been able to do anything well enough for Daddy. I know this sounds like I don't love my daddy, but I do, we just don't see eye to eye on anything. Daddy is a handsome man, and he has those true blue eyes just like my mother. To tell the truth, this has made me wonder about myself, and if I am really my parents daughter. You see I have dark brown eyes, almost ebony, in fact. I asked my mother a long time ago, why my eyes were so dark, and she said her mother had brown eyes, so that is probably why mine are brown.

The doctors' office called today, I guess I will find out something tomorrow. All they would say on the phone, is that the tests are back, and Doctor Browne wants to see me. The waiting room is packed as usual; mother and I can't even find two seats together. I guess that is to be expected though; Doctor Browne is the only M. D. in town. Naturally, my mother will get to go in first to talk with the doctor, it's like they are deciding on how much to tell me, which probably won't be the complete truth. After forever, it seems, I get to talk with Doctor Browne.

"Come right in Suzanna. How are you feeling? How is that voice doing, is it still with you?" he asks.

"Yes sir, the voice is still with me, but I don't think it's that big a deal anymore, do you? I'll bet you have other patients who hear voices."

"No, Suzanna, as a matter of fact, I don't have any other patients with that problem. But no two patients are just alike, as you well know. The blood work shows that you are dangerously anemic, so therefore, I want you to come in every two weeks and get an iron shot. The nurse can give it, so you won't have to make appointments. I'm also going to give you medication to take by mouth each day."

"Then when I get well from anemia Doctor, will that mean the voice will be gone?"

"That I can't say, we will just have to wait and see," he answered.

The nurse gave me my first iron shot, and I could taste it instantly. It's the first shot I've ever had that hurts like the dickens. Getting well is going to take a while I'm afraid, but I surely hope not. On our way home, I asked mother what doctor Browne told her, but just like last time she preferred not to hear me.

"Do you think this will make the voice go away, Mother?"

"Oh, I'm sure it will honey, let's just not talk about the voice anymore, okay?"

The message is loud and clear, my parents think I am crazy, and it's embarrassing for them. I've made a vow to myself, to never mention the voice again to anyone. It's taken close to three months to get over my anemia, and when I saw Doctor Brown the last visit

I lied and told him the voice was gone. I could tell, by looking at his expression, that he was relieved with my answer.

I have a friend, a best friend actually. Her name is Janet. I don't know what I would do without her. We've been friends since the second grade. I think the reason we are such good friends, is because we are opposites. Janet is a vivacious, energetic, and a beautiful person. She loves people and parties--the more people the merrier. She is a true extrovert. I envy her at times, because I am a true introvert. Janet is taller and thinner than me. She has beautiful blue eyes, and lovely light brown hair. She is a great dancer, not me I've got two left feet. Janet has had a tough life really. Her mother died when she was thirteen and her mother's sister, Aunt Missy, took her in. Aunt Missy doesn't have any children of her own; actually she never liked children. She makes life pretty rough for Janet; she never lets Janet forget how much she is doing for her. So in turn, out of guilt, Janet made herself a slave to her Aunt. She did all the heavy housework.

Now that Janet is in high school, her aunt is sending her away, to a private all girl school, just to get her out of her home. Janet says it is understood, that when she graduates, she will be on her own, in other words, she need not even think she can come back here, to live with her aunt. Janet is a really strong person, in spite of her childhood and her aunt. Janet will graduate a year ahead of me, because in the private school, she could double up on subjects and go all year, this makes it possible to get the required credits sooner. Janet came back to our little hometown when she finished school. She went to Atlanta and got a job with the C&S bank. She's rented a room in the little town of Stockbridge, and she rides the Greyhound bus back and forth to work. About six months ago, Janet met Rick, and after dating for three months, they were married. I am still in my last year of high school, and Janet and I have lost contact temporarily.

Chapter Two

Daddy bought me, my very own automobile. I'm sure daddy did this in hopes that I wouldn't get involved with dating. He expects me to go to college, and make something of myself (his own words). He's never even thought about asking me what I would like to do with my life. It's never occurred to him that I might not want to go to college. I have to admit it is great to have my own car. I stop at the drug store soda fountain almost every day after school. Today I was sitting alone, as usual, with my milk shake, when a voice came from behind me.

"May I sit here with you, beautiful," I was afraid to look up, thinking this person can't be talking to me. Then he came around, on my left, and pulled the chair out, proceeding to sit down. I was in shock; this must be the most handsome man in the whole world. Then I looked at him and came up with this dumb question, "Are you talking to me?"

"I surely am, what is your name," he asked?

"My name is Suzanna," I stammered, I'm sure my mouth was hanging open.

"Beautiful name for a beautiful lady. My name is Fred Danvers, do you live around here?"

"Yes, I've lived here most of my life, how about you?"

"Yeah, I grew up here too, but I've been away for a couple of years. Do you work here in town, if so I don't know how I've missed seeing that lovely face, before now?"

"No, I go to high school here, it's my last year in fact." I couldn't believe this gorgeous man was talking to me, and then right out of the blue, he asked, "How about a picture show tonight?"

"Well," I hesitated, but I knew I would have to tell him about my parents' rules.

"You see, my parents have this thing about me dating people they don't know, so I will have to talk to Mother, before I give you an answer."

"Really, how old are you Suzanna?"

I knew right away that he was older than me, and I was afraid he wouldn't want to date a minor, so I lied, "I'm eighteen, why do you ask?"

"Okay, give me your phone number and I will call you later for your answer."

I wrote my phone number on a napkin, with a shaking hand, and gave it to him. He had finished his coke, so he took the napkin and stood to leave.

"See you later doll," and he winked, turned and walked away.

I could hardly wait to get home to talk to Mother. I have always tried to follow the rules of driving, but I didn't even look at the speedometer, as I headed home. I'm most sure that I was speeding. I jumped out of the car, and ran into the house, yelling for my mother like someone insane. "My goodness, what is wrong Suzanna?"

"Nothing is wrong, in fact everything is right. I just met the most handsome man you'll ever see, and he asked me to the picture show tonight. He has the darkest black hair, and the most beautiful blue eyes. I couldn't believe it when he came to my table at the soda fountain, and sat down. Out of all the beautiful girls there, he chose me Mother."

"Just slow down Suzanna, does this person have a name, or were you so excited you forgot to ask him?"

"Sure he has a name, it's Fred Danvers, why do you ask Mother?" Mother wrinkled her brow, and sat down at the kitchen table with me. I knew that look; it meant I was going to be interrogated.

"Is this Fred from around here, is he already out of school, where does he live, and does he have a job if he isn't in school?"

"My gosh, Mother, I didn't get his history, he said he grew up here, but that he's been away a couple of years."

"Away where, Suzanna, prison maybe?" I saw right away that it was pointless to continue our conversation, so I excused myself, and went upstairs to my room.

I heard Daddy when he came in from work, but I didn't go down until Mother called me for the evening meal. I knew if I waited for a while to tell Daddy about Fred that I would lose my nerve completely, so as soon as I settled in my chair I began.

"Daddy do you know the Danvers here in town?" He leaned back in his chair, and a big frown came over his face as he shut his eyes to think. In a few moments he opened his eyes, and looked at me.

"Well, little girl (his name for me since I was a baby), I can't say as I've ever heard of any Danvers here in town, why do you ask?"

"You see while I was at the soda fountain today, I met Fred Danvers, and he said he grew up here. He asked me to go to the picture show with him. I told him I would have to get permission from my parents, before I could give him an answer. He was alright with that, and said he would call me later this evening. So what do you think daddy, can I go out with him?"

"You know we won't allow you to date a stranger Suzanna, he can come here and watch TV with you, while we get to know him. I forbid you to go out of this house with a stranger."

"Why! Daddy that's not fair. Have you ever stopped to think that I'm seventeen, and I haven't ever had a date? I'm not your little girl anymore, look at me Daddy, I'm all grown-up."

I ran out of the kitchen and up the stairs sobbing. Just as I entered the room, my phone rang.

"Hello" I answered, my voice quivering with anger.

"Is this Suzanna?"

"Yes this is Suzanna."

"This is Fred, remember me from this afternoon?"

"Oh yes, Fred, I will go to the picture show with you, but not tonight, because it's a school night, and I have homework to do. I would be happy to go with you on Friday night if that's okay."

"Sure Friday is great, I'll pick you up around six."

"Okay I'll see you then" I replied, and then we said good-bye. I placed the phone on the hook. I was having trouble getting a deep breath. I felt like someone was sitting on my chest. I had never disobeyed my parents before, not deliberately anyway. Right now I will have to go down stairs and try to make things right. If Mother would just once take my side, maybe we could win at least one battle with Daddy. She doesn't seem to mind, being ruled by an iron hand. At times I fail to see, how I could be her daughter, having the feelings I do about independence, and equal rights.

I entered the study, Mother was reading her book, and Daddy was reading his Wall Street Journal, just like every evening of their life. I cleared my throat, and they both looked up.

"We have to discuss something that's important to me, I began."

"So you have our attention little girl," he smiled after saying those words. He knows how to rile me for sure, but I have decided I'm gonna be grown-up about the whole thing.

"A while ago when the phone rang, it was Fred. He was calling for my answer, and I told him I would go with him on Friday to the picture-show. He will be picking me up around six, I wanted y'all to know before Friday."

I could see Daddy's temper flare, his face got blood red. I could feel my knees get weak, while I waited for him to speak.

"How old is this Fred Danvers? Is he married, or did you even ask anything important, tell me what you know about him Suzanna."

"I don't know how old he is, but I'm sure he isn't married."

"How can you be sure he isn't married, if you never asked him? Your mother tells me he said he has been away for two years, away where little girl?"

"I don't know where he was for two years, I didn't think it was any concern of mine. Then my daddy began his speech. "You see little girl older men take advantage of young girls, they have been around and know all the tricks of the trade. They aren't interested in a long-term relationship; they hit and run, so to speak. You have never dated before so you are an older man's dream."

"I may be naive, but I am going out with Fred, and all the talk in the world ain't gonna change my mind, that is how strongly I feel about it Daddy."

I remember now, as I look back, how sad my father looked, as he said to me, "I hope you won't be sorry later, and I truly hope I am wrong about this Fred Danvers."

Chapter Three

Friday is finally here, and I am a nervous wreck. I'm not sure what I should wear, since it's my very first date. I don't want to overdress, but I want to look older. My hair is not at its best, I have just enough curl for my hair to have a mind of its own. I wish I could be a few pounds thinner. I wish I had blue eyes like Fred, instead of these black eyes. I hope Fred won't notice how nervous I am. Mother commented on how nice I looked, when I finally came downstairs. I hope she wasn't just trying to put me at ease. I'm sure it's only natural that she would feel that way; after all she is my mother.

Fred drove up to the house and blew the horn, this really upset my mother, but I ran for the front door, before she could voice her opinion.

"Don't you look terrific," said Fred, as I slid into the car. I blushed and was lost for words. Finally I said thank you, almost in a whisper.

"As good looking as you are Suzanna, I'll bet you have a date book full of admirers. I looked at him to see if he was making fun. It seemed he meant it.

"No, actually this is my very first date. I haven't been interested in dating anyone in school; they all seem so immature. I've never met anyone out of school, until you of course."

"So, it sounds like you prefer older guys." "I've never given it any thought, but I do like a person to be more mature than most of my classmates."

"Okay Suzanna, you stick with me, and I'll teach you everything I know."

When we were on our way back to my house Fred asked me if he could see me again the next night. He said we could go out for dinner, and play it by ear the rest of the evening. I was beside myself; I never dreamed he would ask me out two nights in a row. We arrived at my house, he got out and opened my door, and then he walked me to the front porch. He touched my arm when we got to the steps, I turned to look at him, when I did he drew me close into his arms. I felt his lips on mine. The kiss was so long I felt like I would just faint. He released me and whispered, "I'll see you tomorrow night." I rushed into the house, and ran up the stairs to my room. I couldn't wait to be alone to relive the night over again. I have never been kissed before, but I just know I have found my soul mate. I remember Mother telling me that love comes to those who wait. At the time she told me this I was feeling down, because I didn't think I would ever have my first date. Believe me I didn't believe what she said at that time. You know though, I think mothers are a lot smarter than we give them credit for.

Chapter Four

Fred came for me tonight, but he still just blew the horn, instead of coming to the door. My mother says this is disrespectful, that a gentleman wouldn't blow his horn for his date. Mother said he would come to the door, to escort his date to the car. Then he would proceed to open the car door for her. It's been years since my mother dated, so that might have been just the era. Today is just different.

Fred took me to the only restaurant we have in this little town. We ordered steak, and Fred ordered red wine. I told him right away that I didn't drink alcohol, that I would like iced tea. He laughed at me, "dear Suzanna don't you know that you can't get inebriated on wine?" I don't know anything about alcohol, but then I remember in the bible at The Last Supper, Jesus drank wine, so I guess it is alright. While we were eating, Fred kept refilling my glass, and I kept drinking it, like a ninny. When I stood up to leave the restaurant, I felt dizzy. I wasn't sure I could walk, but then Fred took my arm and escorted me to the car.

"What would you like to do now, my sweet Suzanna?"

I don't care, what would you like to do?"

Then he said: "Okay, why don't we go to my apartment and listen to some music. Maybe dance a little too, what you say Suzanna?"

"I'm not sure we should do that Fred, my folks wouldn't approve of me going to your apartment."

"So what, they'll never know, Suzanna, who's gonna tell them, I'm not."

"I guess it would be okay, but we can't stay too long, you know I have to be home by twelve o'clock."

"What! This is Saturday night, are you sure you are eighteen years old. Whoever heard of a woman of age, having to be home by midnight? On a week-end night, at that?"

"I'm the kind of person who respects my parents, and I will respect them even when I'm twenty-five years old."

When we entered the apartment, I could hardly believe my eyes. Everything was neat and clean as a pin. In fact it was lots neater than my room. It was located upstairs in one of the many old Victorian homes in town. It had stairs outside the main house, leading to the apartment for privacy. I asked Fred if he had a housekeeper. He laughed and said, I wish. He said he had learned neatness when he was in the marines.

"So that's where you were for two years,"

"Yes, where did you think I was, in prison or something?" I felt my face flush, "no of course not."

Fred crossed the room to select a record for the player. I walked over to look through his collection. He had a great selection of slow dance records. He held me close and we were barely moving, that was okay with me, because I still didn't feel steady on my feet. He softly sang along with the record. I had to be excused, and while I was in the bathroom, Fred opened a bottle of wine. He had already chilled the glasses in the freezer, this should have raised a red flag for me, but it didn't.

We sat on the couch and sipped our wine. I asked Fred if he was sure a person couldn't get intoxicated on wine. "Oh no, you might get a little buzz, and feel really good, but you would never get inebriated on wine."

"I don't feel well, I think you should take me home Fred."

"Come with me," he said, holding me up, he led me to the bedroom.

"No," I said, "I can't lay on your bed, it wouldn't be right."

"Who says it's not right, he whispered in my ear, as he lay me back on the pillows." When he started to unbutton my blouse, I began to cry.

"Please don't," I whispered, "I'm a virgin." I don't remember what happened after that, it must have been over an hour later when I woke up. I stumbled to the bathroom, I was so sick. I lost most of the wine. I got up from the floor to find a washcloth for my face. Fred stepped into the room and took the cloth, and began to bathe my face. I pushed him away, and told him not to touch me. He laughed and said: "Don't play little Miss innocent with me, you knew why we came to my apartment. You also know there is no such thing as an eighteen year old virgin." The tears ran down my cheeks while I told Fred the truth.

"I'm only seventeen, and you know I was a virgin, and I begged you to stop. I hate you and I want you to take me home right now!" Fred gripped my arm and turned me around to face him. "Let me tell you something, you had better keep your mouth shut about what happened here tonight, if you know what's good for you. Do you understand me, Suzanna?" I looked him in the eye, and I slowly replied: "I would never tell anyone, not because I'm afraid of what you might do, but because I am so ashamed of what happened. I wish I had never laid eyes on you, Fred Danvers." He drove me home in complete silence. When he pulled into my driveway, I got out of the car and ran, not even giving him a backward glance. I felt so dirty. I stood in the shower, and tried to wash my skin off, but I still didn't feel clean. I didn't want to return to school on Monday. I felt that one could look at me and know what I had done. I will never tell a soul about this, not even my best friend Janet.

Spring is here and I'm feeling so much better. After my episode with Fred, all my attention is being applied to my studies, and my reward is I'll be graduating with honors. The stress from the relationship took my appetite, and I have lost so much weight that I'm almost thin. I have a new hairstyle, which I think is becoming. My naturally curly hair has always been hard to control. I had come to the conclusion that I would just let it go its own way. Then I found someone who knows how to cut with the curl, and it's much easier to style now.

Chapter Five

My friend Janet is happily married and expecting her first child soon. I've been thinking, since I have the whole summer ahead of me, that I might offer to help Janet with the baby for a while, at least until she feels able to do the housework, etc. Mother says it's a good thing, and would let Janet know that I will always be there for her. As close as Janet and I have been over the years, I'm sure she already knows I will always be there, when she needs me. Janet thinks I should find someone and settle down and have a family. I understand that she only wants happiness for me, but I'm not sure I will ever want to be married. I can't comprehend spending the rest of my life, with one person. Till death do us part, could be a long, long time.

The baby is here, it's a girl, and Janet named her Jane Marie. I have moved in with Janet and her husband Rick, to help out. It's a small two-bedroom apartment, and I sleep on a day bed in the babies' room. Jane is a beautiful baby and a good baby too. Janet says being a mother is a feeling one can't put into words. She also reminded me how we had always planned to have our families together. We also hoped, maybe our daughters would become best friends, just like we are. I do remember but I reminded her that I don't even have a boyfriend.

"I know but there are lots of single men living in this very complex. You should hang out at the pool, I'll bet you could meet someone nice, and good-looking."

"I'm here to help you out, not to look for a boyfriend, for goodness' sake listen to yourself Janet."

"There isn't that much to do, to help me around here, Suzanna you have just gotta try it, just once for me please."

"I don't know Janet, I'm not that crazy about swimming, and I really don't like the sun that much."

"Suzanna, you've got to stop being so shy. Since you've lost all that weight, you have a terrific figure, although I didn't see anything wrong with you before."

"Okay Janet I'll think about it, but don't push me."

"Good that's what I want you to do, to be thinking about it," said Janet.

Janet finally gave up on Suzanna finding her Mr. Right. She decided that she would just have to take it upon herself, to find the right partner, for her friend. After all, she didn't do half bad choosing her own mate. Surely Ricky knew some single guys at work, she would ask him tonight. Janet and Rick were in bed. They had made a habit of waiting until all was quiet, to have their talk about their day. This was the ideal time for Janet to ask Rick about the guys he worked with every day. Suzanna and the baby were already asleep.

"Ricky, do you know any single men at work?"

"Sure honey, why?"

"I want Suzanna to meet someone nice; she needs a man in her life."

"But honey, there are single men all over this complex. Don't you think if Suzanna wanted someone in her life, she would go out and find her own?"

"I've tried to get her to go to the pool, but she's just too shy."

"That's hard for me to believe, with you two being best friends, Janet."

"I know Rick, I've never talked to you about Suzanna. She has some emotional problems, which no one seems to understand, not even me. She really doesn't bear her soul to anyone. I know she's lonely, but she would never admit it. She's the best listener that one could ever meet; however she doesn't discuss her inner feelings. She would give you her last dollar, but would never ask you for anything."

"Yeah honey, I know what you mean, she is different from anyone I've ever known. I don't mean any harm by this, but she is a little odd, in my book."

"Maybe you could invite one of your single friends to supper one night, not just anyone now, someone you know who is really a nice guy. How about it?"

"Well now let me think, Rick mumbled to himself, why yeah come to think of it there is Bill Norton. He's probably the nicest guy

I know, I've never heard him even say a curse word.

I've never seen him get angry. He's just a laid back, all around good person."

"Great, squealed Janet, see if Bill would like to come to supper Friday night. Find out if he already has a girlfriend first of course, if he doesn't tell him about Suzanna."

"Tell him what about Suzanna?"

"O you know, how attractive, and how interesting she is to be around. Tell him she doesn't have a steady boyfriend right now, you know, that kind of stuff."

"Okay I'll do it just for you, now let me get some shut eye. I do have to work tomorrow you know,"

Janet and I were having coffee when Janet casually mentioned that one of Rick's friends was coming over for supper.

"Oh, I'll just go on home for the weekend then," I replied.

"No you won't! You are the reason I asked Rick, to ask Bill over in the first place."

"Janet, why would you do that? Who is Bill anyway? What if we don't have anything in common?"

"So be it, if that happens, it's not the end of the world, Suzanna. You never go anywhere to meet anyone. You haven't been down to the pool not once, although you said you would think about it. I don't know how you expect to ever meet anyone, just sitting in this apartment with me, day in and day out."

"I've got plenty of time Janet, it's not like I'm an old maid. Anyway, I'm thinking about going to college, at least a couple of years."

"Why haven't you told me Suzanna, I'm so thrilled for you, why I think that's just wonderful."

"I don't know Janet; I really don't know what I want to do, for sure. I feel like my life is standing still, and time is moving on without me."

"Suzanna, I don't understand you, you have everything. A mother and father who love you and gives you anything your heart desires. Your choices are unlimited. I would settle for just a loving mother and daddy, myself. Maybe you've had too much, Suzanna."

"You know Janet, I'm happy for you that you are happily

married, however it doesn't mean I can't be happy not married."

"I know Suzanna, but you don't know what you are missing. Not having someone to love and care for you. You can't imagine what a wonderful feeling it is, to bring a new life into this world."

"I'm just not ready for marriage Janet. I'm not sure I will ever be, and I'm not sure I want to be committed to anyone for the rest of my life. I feel a great need to be free. You are married now, and you can't always do what you want, not without talking it over with Rick anyway. I've had my mother and father telling me what I can and can't do for eighteen years, and I don't need to replace them with a husband. When Rick's friend comes over tonight, please don't push him on me, or vice-versa, do you understand what I'm saying Janet?"

"Sure I understand, and I hope you don't think I'm trying to tell you what to do, because I wouldn't dream of doing such a thing. It's just that you never let you guard down completely, not even with me, and I've been your friend for years. I've bared my soul to you, but I don't think I even know you at times, Suzanna. It's like you don't feel you can trust anyone, even your very best friend. I wish you would give me a chance to be the friend to you that you are to me."

"Trust me Janet, you are my friend. You have been there for me over the years, just as I have for you. You of all people, after all these years, should understand that I'm a very private person, by nature. It's not that I don't trust you, I don't trust the feelings I have within, that's why I can't share everything with you."

"I'm sorry if inviting Rick's friend over for supper is stepping over the line of our friendship. I should have asked you first. If you don't want to be here for supper I'll understand."

"Oh, don't be silly Janet, it's okay. Now let's get in the kitchen and decide what to fix."

Chapter Six

We sat down to eat; Bill sat directly across from me. He is tall and dark and yes, he is a handsome man. His voice is soft and mellow. He is shy and he doesn't have much to say; however Janet and Rick are taking care of the conversation. I think I would like to get to know Bill, he seems sensitive and attentive. There is a gentleness about him, and I feel I already know him somehow.

After we finished the meal we moved into the living room with our coffee and desert. Just as we sat down little Jane began to cry. Janet and Rick excused themselves to see about the baby. Both of them had never gone to see about Jane, before to my knowledge. It was evident what was going on, this would force Bill and I to get acquainted. In my heart I was thankful to Janet for leaving us alone.

Bill broke the silence with a question, "do you work Suzanna?"

"No I'm considering going to college in the fall, so I think I'll just laze around this summer."

"I think that's great, I couldn't afford to go to college, but I'm hoping somewhere in the future I will be able to go nights."

Bill asked me to go to a drive-in movie the next Friday.

Before I knew what I was saying, I told him I would love to go.

"I'll pick you up at six, if that will be okay."

"Sure you can pick me up here. If you would like to come earlier, we could go for a swim, and maybe grill some burgers."

"That sounds good, about what time should I be here, is there anything I need to bring?"

"Around five will be fine, and it won't be necessary for you to bring anything."

When Janet and Rick entered the room they were full of apologies, as if they didn't leave us alone on purpose.

I was getting ready for bed, when Janet knocked on the door.

"Come on in."

"Tell me Suzanna, that Bill is a looker, don't you think?"

"Yes as a matter of fact he is, and he asked me out next Friday night. I took the liberty to ask him to come for a cookout here and maybe a swim, before we go to the show. I hope you and Rick won't mind."

"You know we don't mind, we wanted you two to get together, as you already know. Oh Suzanna, maybe Bill is Mr. Right, wouldn't that be wonderful? Y'all could get an apartment right here in our complex, and we could be neighbors."

"Good grief, Janet, you have marring on the brain. I've only just met the man, and you have us married. I'm not ready to marry anyone. Before I even consider getting married, I want to leave my mark on the world somehow; so when I die my memory will live on."

"Suzanna, when you get married, you have children to carry on your memory. When you grow old, you have children to take care for you, if need be. I just don't know where you are coming from, would you please explain it to me?"

"Janet, I'm just saying, I want to be somebody in this world. I want to find out who I am, and what I need, to become a whole person. I feel so mixed up inside, it's like I am a stranger to myself. You will never understand me, if I can't understand myself."

"Come on Suzanna, don't get dramatic with me, I'm your best friend, remember?"

"No Janet, you are my only friend; we both know that. I'm your best friend, but you do have other friends, and I'm happy for you. So just be truthful, and admit to me that I am different from anyone else you know, maybe I'm just a little bit crazy, huh?"

"Why Suzanna, that's the dumbest thing I've ever heard you say. We both know that you aren't crazy. Where in this world did you get an idea like that? Why don't we go to bed now, and we'll talk about this again tomorrow, when we are all rested and refreshed, okay?"

The next morning Janet asked me how I was feeling. I told her I felt fine, but she looked awful.

Then she told me she couldn't sleep for thinking about the things we discussed the night before.

She told me she thought I should see a doctor about my problem. She told me if she knew how to help me she would, but she felt I needed a professional. This put me on the defensive, and I gave Janet the whole spill about women of today, and how they felt about just being housewives and mothers. I told her thinking the way she did about family and marriage was obsolete. I upset her and she gave me her spill about how the life she had chosen makes her happy, how she doesn't have any desire to go out to work in the world.

"Suzanna," she said, "it would be great to have more money, but it isn't the end of the world if I never have more than I have now. To me, happiness is the most important thing in life. You for instance, have had everything you ever wanted, a successful dad, a loving mother, a beautiful home, and plenty of money. You sit here and say, you don't know who you are, or what you want. Suzanna I don't believe you believe what you are saying. I think you are searching for happiness. I know you are not insane. I do think, to get to the bottom of your problem, you need professional help. Please think about this, I only tell you this, because I love you like a sister."

When Janet finished her speech, tears were streaming down her cheeks. We embraced and our tears flowed freely. I knew in my heart that Janet was right.

Friday is finally here and Bill will be arriving soon. Janet has been a nervous wreck all day, trying to be sure everything is just perfect.

"Suzanna, will you check again and make sure we have everything for the cookout? I would be so embarrassed if we have to ask the guys to go to the store for something at the last minute."

"Sure, I'll check for the umpteenth time," I answered. "I don't know why you are so nervous; after all he is my date. Why don't you just sit down and relax? After all it's not Bill's first visit, you didn't make this much fuss then."

"Suzanna, can't you understand, I want this to be a perfect evening for you. Please give Bill a fair chance. Try not to judge him too quickly. I know you don't want to hear this, but you know he could be your soul mate."

"Janet I'm just going to be myself, okay. If he likes me, maybe he will ask me out again, if not, nothing is lost. I'm going to go freshen up if you don't mind. I heard the doorbell just as I finished brushing my hair. Rick was showing Bill to a seat when I entered the living room. Bill rose as I entered the room.

"I'm glad you could come early Bill, did you bring your swim suite? I thought maybe we could go down to the pool before we eat, that would be better than after, don't you think?"

"Sure I'll just run down to the car and get my trunks," he answered. I went to change into my swim suite. Maybe if we have a little time alone, I can learn more about Bill before we leave for the show. I never intend to let another Fred into my life, never.

Bill returned and headed for the bathroom to put on his trunks. I asked Janet, not to start cooking until I returned to help.

"Nonsense," she answered. "Rick will come get you two when everything is ready. We don't need any help, cooking hamburgers. Y'all run on and enjoy your swim."

We swam the length of the pool, Bill could see how winded I was, so he suggested we sit on the side of the pool and talk for a while. We sat dangling our feet in the water.

"Well Bill as you can see, I'm not that good a swimmer. I love the feel of the water; it's so silky against my skin. I never had swimming lessons, so I don't know the proper way to breath and etc. Daddy tells me I try to knock all the water out of the pool, just to keep my face out of the water. He tried to give me some pointers when I was younger, but I could never live up to his expectations, in anything I tried to do."

"Your dad sounds like a perfectionist."

"You got it, that's my daddy all right. I don't think I've done one thing that was good enough for him, he has never, not once told me, he is proud of me. Oh well, enough about my daddy; let's change the subject to something interesting. If you don't mind my asking Bill, how old are you?" "I just turned twenty-one"

"What kind of work do you do?"

"I'm in data processing, and I enjoy my work."

"How did you know what kind of work you would enjoy Bill?"

"I didn't know until I went to the IBM school. My parents couldn't afford to send me to college. Daddy is a laborer, and I knew I wanted something better. As the years go by and dad gets older, his job gets harder physically, which he has pointed out to all us kids."

"How many siblings do you have?"

"There's eight of us, four boys and four girls, and I'm the oldest."

"How many in your family, Suzanna?"

27

"Just me, I always thought it would be fun to have brothers and sisters. My mother came from a big family; I guess that's why she only had me. I'll bet it's interesting to be part of a big family." "It can be fun at times, but most of the time it is hectic. I don't think you are missing that much not having a big family. There is never any privacy. There's always noise and quarreling, and just general chaos. So consider yourself lucky Suzanna, I can understand your mother's reasoning, especially since she's from a large family."

"I wonder if I could ask you another personal question, Bill?"

"Sure I guess so."

"Do you drink alcohol?"

"Uh-uh, I never could see the point in drinking, not knowing what you might do or say could be embarrassing. I guess it might be alright if one knew when they had, had enough, but most every one I know who drinks, just don't know when to stop. Personally, I like to know when I'm having a good time, and I never have any money to throw away."

"I've noticed you don't smoke either do you?" I asked.

"I think smoking is a big waste of money. I just never seemed to have time to smoke, I guess it's alright for some people, but I feel like it's also a waste of time as well as money."

I looked up and saw Ricky on his way down," here comes Rick, I guess it's time to dry off, and go eat, are you ready?"

"Sure I've worked up an appetite, and I have enjoyed the swim, and the conversation," Bill answered.

We met Rick and headed for the patio. The evening cook out was enjoyable, and Janet didn't get pushy, thank goodness. I had never gone to a drive-in movie with a guy that is. I had been a few times with my parents, but I felt myself getting a little tense when we parked. After we had been there a good while, I began to relax, for I realized that Bill was truly a gentleman. He didn't ever even try to touch me, which made my evening enjoyable. On our way back home, we stopped at this little place called the Spinning Wheel, and we had milk shakes. It was my first time to have curb-service, which I thought was neat, not having to get out of the car to make your order.

I told Bill how much I had enjoyed the evening. He said it had been good for him too, and he would like to see me again I told him it would be a pleasure to go out with him again, however I thought it would only be fair to tell him that I was not ready for a relationship with anyone at this time. I told him I needed time to decide what I wanted to do with my life.

"I can live with that, he said. Do you know you are so comfortable to be with? What I mean is I've never felt this much at ease with any other girl I've known. My first date with a girl is usually stressful, but it's like I've known you always." I told him that I felt at ease with him also.

"Then we are good friends for now, okay?" he said.

"That sounds just fine to me," I answered. "It's getting so late, I wonder if you could drop me off at my house, instead of Janet's place? I need to get some more clothes and things, over the weekend."

"Sure just tell me how to get there," said Bill.

I felt an uneasiness in Bill as he walked me to the door. He kissed me on the cheek, and said goodnight.

A feeling of sadness spread over Bill as he drove home. The huge house Suzanna lived in intimidated him, because he is from such a humble home, compared to hers. I'm glad we decided to be just good friends, he thought, I could never offer her the things she's used to. I guess deep down, I was hoping she was the one for me, but I know now, she's way out of my reach. Maybe I should just let it go, and not call her again, however she has been up front with me, and I did promise to be her friend.

While I was getting dressed for bed, I couldn't help but have mixed feeling for Bill. Maybe I shouldn't have asked him to bring me to my house tonight. It seemed to upset him somehow, I could feel the tension building, as he drove up our driveway. He seemed taken aback with my home, and I think that's why he became awkward. I hope this won't ruin things for us as friends. If he doesn't call me anymore, I'm really going to miss him.

Chapter Seven

Rick looked up at the cafeteria line and saw Bill. He wondered why Bill was here, because he usually brought his lunch, and ate in the break room. When Bill got through the line, he started straight for Rick's table. He stopped opposite Rick and placed his tray on the table.

"Do you have time to talk with me Rick, or are you looking for someone else to join you?" "Nah man, I'm not expecting anyone, have a seat. What's wrong Bill?"

"I need to talk to you about Suzanna. Why didn't you tell me she comes from a wealthy family? When I took her home Friday night, I wasn't prepared for a neighborhood like that, and that big old house she lives in. I would have never asked her out if I had know. Rick, I don't have anything to offer someone like her. I just assumed, since she was staying over at your place, that she was like you and me."

"Now just hold your horses man, Suzanna is just an ordinary person. She's been Janet's best friend since their childhood. You are right, her folks have plenty, but Suzanna is not a snob."

"Rick, that's not what I'm saying, I realize Suzanna is not a snob, if that had been the case, I would have never asked her out. The thing that's bothering me is I'm getting some strong feelings for her, like I've never had with anyone else. You and I know that it wouldn't be wise for me to fall in love with her. It's just plain to see that Suzanna is from a different world, a world that I could never feel comfortable in."

"Look buddy, I introduced you two, because Janet insisted. You happen to be the most decent friend I have. If you want to lay the blame on someone, then lay it on Janet. She has this weird notion that Suzanna needs someone to watch over her, emotionally or whatever. Janet has this way about her that makes her think she can fix the whole world. I guess you could say, she thinks she is Cupid in the flesh."

"Suzanna told me she's not ready for any kind of commitment, I figure the last person she was with must have hurt her real bad, is that what happened, Rick?"

"I have no idea about that Bill, so what's the problem? Seems to me if she made it clear she isn't looking for something permanent you should be able to go out and have fun for as long as you two want to be together."

"You're not reading me, Rick, the problem is I'm afraid I'll fall in love with her, then what?"

"Okay Bill, you do whatever you want to do. You don't have to take Suzanna out anymore, that's completely up to you. You know it won't hurt our friendship, either way."

"Hey Rick, don't mention anything I've said to Janet. I wouldn't want it to get back to Suzanna. I do want to keep seeing her. I don't know if I can be as relaxed with her as before, but I did promise her I would be her friend for now."

"Bill you don't have to keep that promise, if you think you're gonna be hurt later."

"I'm a man of my word, and I will keep my promise. If I get hurt it will be my own doing."

"I'm really sorry about this whole thing Bill, I wish you the best man, and don't worry, I won't say a word about this to Janet."

"Come on in the kitchen Suzanna, sit here at the table, I'll get us a coke." Janet brought the cokes and sat down across from me. The kitchen is our favorite place to visit.

"Now tell me about your date with Bill, don't leave out one thing. I need to know every little thing that was said."

"The date was perfect, he is a true gentleman. After the drive in, we stopped at this quaint little place called the Spinning Wheel; we had curb service, which I've never done before. We had a delicious milk shake. It was then I told Bill that I was not ready for a relationship with anyone at this time. I told him I would be happy to be a friend, and he told me that seemed fair enough to him. He also would like to be friends. When he walked me to the door, he gave me a friendly little peck on the cheek, and said he would call me later."

"Are you telling me that you didn't get any kind of feelings for that adorable man, other than wanting to be his friend? You must have ice water in those veins of yours, that's all I have to say."

"You are not listening to me Janet. I like Bill a lot, but I don't plan to lead him on, since I don't know if I could follow through. You see Janet, Bill is a very sensitive and gentle person, and I wouldn't hurt him for the world. What I'm saying is, I don't want him to fall in love with me."

"What brings you to this conclusion, are you saying that you know you couldn't love Bill?"

"No, I'm saying I'm not good enough for him, Janet. I have a way of hurting people, the ones I love the most actually. I refuse to be the one to hurt Bill."

"Suzanna, where do you get such dumb ideas? You have to stop putting yourself down. After all you are a very sensitive person too, and I know you well enough to know that you would never deliberately hurt anyone. Suzanna you need to get professional help, to find out what is eating you alive. I am here to help you all I can, but I don't have the answers to your problems. I will always be here to listen, but that's all I can give you. Promise me that you will seek help, you are dear to me, and I want you to find happiness, because you deserve happiness."

I decided to follow Janet's suggestion. The next morning I called and made an appointment with dear old doc Browne. I hadn't taken my seat good, in his office, before he asked me if I was hearing the voice again. "No sir, I lied, but I feel so out of control. I feel as though I'm floating above myself, and looking down on myself. I see myself as a complete stranger. I came to see you to ask if you could recommend a psychiatrist Dr Browne. I didn't think it would be wise to just pick one from the yellow pages."

"Yes I know a good doctor," said Dr Browne, "but do your parents know you are here and why you came?"

"No sir, I'm afraid they might not understand. I was thinking maybe you could talk to Mother and Daddy for me."

"Okay," Dr Browne replied, as he rose from his chair, I'll talk to them and then I'll get back to you."

I asked the doctor how long it would take to set up an appointment for me. His answer was: not long, that is once I convince your parents it's necessary. He said he was glad that I realized I needed help, that that in itself is half the cure. He also said that he had suggested this to my parents, back when I was hearing the voice. When I inquired why my parents didn't follow his advice, he told me they preferred to believe it was just a stage I was going through, a part of growing up. He said my parents were in denial; they refused to believe their child could possibly need mental help.

I asked him what would I do if they still would not agree. He told me that now I am of age, and I really don't need their consent. Even so, I told him I would feel much better, if he would talk to Mother and Daddy, and try to get them to see that I do need help. They must know by now, it's not just a stage I'm going through. Doctor Browne told me he would do his best to make them see my need. He told me not to worry, that he felt sure he would be calling me soon.

While I was driving home, I tried to calm myself, but I couldn't think about anything else. I wonder what doctor Browne knows. He made the statement that I have been needing help for years. I wish I knew what he told Mother and Daddy, why had they been so stubborn and secretive about it?

Maybe if they had taken the doctor's advice, I would be well by now. What if it's too late now, and whatever is wrong can't be fixed? What if there is no hope for me now? Maybe I should just forget the whole thing, if Mother and Daddy are afraid of the truth, then maybe I should be too.

* * *

When Frank came home from work, he found Mary in tears. She was so upset that she hadn't ever started dinner, which was unheard of as far as Frank was concerned. It was the first time Frank could remember in their whole marriage that his supper wasn't ready when he walked in the house from work each evening. He found Mary lying across their bed.

"Honey, what in the world is wrong?" he asked.

"Oh Frank, Doctor Browne called here today. He said Suzanna came by to see him yesterday, and she asked him to recommend a psychiatrist for her. He asked if you and I could come in and discuss the matter. Oh Frank, what are we going to do?"

"Well honey, I guess we will go in to see the doctor. If he feels she needs help, then we will get help for her."

"What if Suzanna finds out the secret when she gets help? It will ruin our lives, including her own, you know that Frank."

"Mary, Mary, there is no way a shrink will find out anything that Suzanna doesn't know already about herself. Frankly if you want my opinion, I don't believe those doctors can help anyone. I think it's a gimmick, people need someone to listen to them, then they feel better, after they unload all their grievances, and they think the doctor is helping them."

"Oh! I do hope you are right Frank. We should have told Suzanna years ago, and all this wouldn't be happening to us now."

"Mary we did what we thought was best back then, and it's too late now to do anything about it."

The next afternoon Frank and Mary went to talk with doctor Browne. Frank began: "Do you have anyone in mind to see Suzanna, doctor? Mary and I have talked it over, and if you agree a psychiatrist can solve Suzanna's problems, whatever they are, then you have our permission to go ahead."

"I feel," answered the doctor, "that if Suzanna feels the need, then a good doctor can surely help her. You see the first step of emotional or mental problems, is the person admitting to themselves that they have the problem."

"Suzanna doesn't have a mental problem, does she? Mary asked. I know she had that voice thing, but I thought that was caused by her being so seriously anemic."

"No Mary, I never told you that, you chose to believe what you wanted to believe."

"But doctor you gave her medication for the problem, did you not?" cried Mary.

"I wish we did have medication for voices, but we don't," said doctor Browne.

"Why didn't you tell us this at the time?" asked Frank.

"If y'all remember, I suggested that Suzanna be hospitalized if the problem persisted. You both disagreed, strongly. You both preferred to think it was her age along with changes in hormones, and everything would take care of itself. I think it's time for us to face the truth. Suzanna does have a serious problem, which she even recognizes. I have a good friend in the field of psychiatry, and I believe he can help her. His name is Richard Shannon, and he's in the doctor's building on Peachtree Street, in Atlanta. Should I go ahead and make Suzanna an appointment with him?"

"Yes and we thank you for your concern," said Frank.

"Frank, Mary, could I ask you if either of you have any idea what is wrong with Suzanna? Could it be something that happened when she was very young? Perhaps before y'all moved here? My records show that I started seeing Suzanna when she was about four years old."

"We don't have the vaguest idea. Her childhood was perfectly normal. We are just at our rope's end, trying to figure out what her problem is." said Frank.

On their way home, Mary began to cry. "You see I told you Frank. Even doctor Browne is suspicious of us."

"Mary you have to get control of yourself. What Suzanna doesn't know can't be the cause of her sickness. Maybe it's in her genes or something, maybe we will never know, but you have to stop blaming yourself. If you don't it will make you sick too. Now the subject is closed, all we can do is hope that doctor Shannon can at least make Suzanna think he is helping her.

Chapter Eight

I walked into doctor Shannon's office, not knowing what to expect. It was elegant. The furniture was genuine leather, but I didn't see a couch anywhere. In all the picture shows I had seen, the patient always lay on a couch, and the doctor took notes on his little yellow pad. Well so much for Hollywood, huh. Doctor Shannon rose from his chair, behind a huge mahogany desk, to shake my hand. I saw his credentials hanging on the wall. They were quite impressive; there were at least four different diplomas, from four different universities.

"Hello, Suzanna, I'm doctor Robert Shannon. You may call me Robert if you choose, please be seated."

I took a seat on a big leather chair, clasping my hands tightly, surprisingly I was a nervous wreck. I couldn't even get a deep breath; I had never felt this way before. I thought I might panic any minute.

"Just sit back and relax he said, there is nothing to be afraid of, I hope we can become the best of friends in time. Let's just get acquainted on this first visit. How long have you been doctor Browne's patient?"

"I've been going to doctor Browne almost all my life I recalled. We moved to Henry County when I was around four years old, and since he's the only doctor in town, he's been my physician ever since."

"Tell me how you feel right this minute, right off the top of your head, Suzanna."

"I feel lost, I can't seem to fit in anywhere. It's as though I have a big void inside, but I can't seem to fill that void, no matter how I try."

"Do you get along with both your parents?"

"Oh yes, my parents are great, I have always had anything I wanted. The only real complaint I have is that at times they are overprotective."

"Do you think your parents love you?"

"Yes I think in their own way they love me, but I don't think they understand me."

"Why do you say they don't understand you?"

"All my life it seems, or as far back as I can recall anyway, they've treated me as though I am not capable of making a decision. They try to change my feelings about everything. They don't think I ever know what's best for me."

"Give me an example Suzanna, so I can better understand what you're saying."

"Okay, that'll be easy enough. Once when I was around ten years old, I wanted to paint my room orchid, but no, Mother said that I would be sick of the color within a month. She said I would be limited in other colors to mix and match. She thought it would be much better to keep it blue or maybe we could paint it pink. I knew we wouldn't be able to change the color at all, unless my daddy agreed to it, and I figured she just didn't want to discuss it with him. She would have had to have dozens of reasons to sell him on it."

"I hear you saying that your father always has the last word in your home, right?"

"Absolutely right, Mother never lets me go anywhere, or do anything without talking it over with Daddy first."

"You resent this control don't you, Suzanna?"

"Yes, I surely do, and it makes me angry that my mother allows him to tell her what to do also. He chooses the clothes she wears, even what colors are best for her, in his opinion anyway.

Doctor I just feel like a misfit, I don't know how to make friends, that's not true, I do know how. I just enjoy being alone more than being with others. I suppose you will say that's not normal, but that's my true feelings."

"Suzanna it's almost impossible to define the word normal, as you probably already know. What's normal for one person might not be considered normal for another. I see nothing wrong in you enjoying being alone. Did you know there are people who are afraid to be alone, even for just a little while? Although everyone should spend some of their time with others. When we are with other people it's educational, because we learn from each other. Do you agree?"

"Yes that makes sense to me, when you put it that way, but I need my own little world. I feel completely safe in my world. I feel incomplete in the outside world. I feel there is something missing that is important to make me a whole person. I can't explain it; there is a hole inside me, which I can't fill, because I don't know what to fill it with. I know I'm not making any sense to you, but it's the best I can do. You know Doctor; I can't remember being a child. My best friend can remember things that happened to her, when she was just two years old." I can't remember being even, before I started school. What causes this Dr Shannon?"

"I'll tell you what, we will pick up with that question on your next visit. I'll make a note of it here, and I'll see you at the same time next week. We will find some answers Suzanna, so you just relax and keep your chin up, okay?"

I left the office confused and doubtful. I don't feel any better about things. I guess it might take a lot longer than I anticipated, to feel better about myself. When I arrived home I barely got my foot in the door, before Mother ran and grabbed my arm to drag me into the kitchen. She was stammering like a hyper child, I have no idea why she is acting this way, and a nervous wreck. "Sit down here with me, and tell me all about your visit to Dr Shannon, dear."

"There is not all that much to tell Mother, I don't feel any better about myself, than I did before I met the doctor. Since I don't know what is wrong with me, I don't know what to ask him."

Honey, that's what he's there for, to find out what is wrong. I don't think you have to know the right questions to ask. Do you like him, as a person?"

"Yes as a matter of fact I do like him personally, but I'm not sure he is taking me seriously."

"Why do you think he doesn't take you seriously, Suzanna?"

"I don't know why, Mother, it's just a feeling I have. I think I'll go over and visit with Janet. Don't fix dinner for me; I might stay the night."

I knocked on Janet's door, but I didn't hear anyone inside. I opened the door and stuck my head in and yelled," is there anyone home?" I heard her voice coming from the bedroom.

"Yes Suzanna, come on in I'll be right with you, "Little Bit" has had an accident and we are in the bathroom." Jane Marie is a petite little thing, and Janet and Rick have given her the nickname, "Little

Bit," which I think is appropriate in this case, even though I usually don't like nicknames. Once we were seated in the kitchen, Janet wanted to know what I had been doing.

"I had my first appointment with Dr Shannon this morning," was my answer.

"You did! Suzanna, do you think he can help you?"

"I don't know, it's like I told Mother, I can't explain my feelings very well, so I don't see how he will be able to help me that much. I don't know exactly what I expect him to do for me in the first place."

"My goodness, Suzanna, he's been trained to know how to help you. If you know what is wrong with you, you don't need his help. Now don't start worrying about this."

"You are absolutely right Janet, I'm not gonna give it another thought, that's Dr Shannon's job now."

"Good, now how are things going with you and Bill?"

"Bill hasn't called in over a week now, I figure he's just not interested anymore."

"There you go again Suzanna, putting yourself down. I just don't know what we're gonna do with you. You do know that you need to give yourself a good talking too, I hope."

"Okay enough about me Janet, what have you and Rick been doing lately, anything interesting?"

"Not a whole lot of anything, "Little Bit" has been impossible with her teething in this hot weather. We haven't even had time to just sit down and talk to each other. Ricky has been grumpy lately; I guess he's just not getting enough rest, or maybe it's the heat."

"Y'all need to take a weekend trip somewhere Janet, it would be good for both of you to have some time alone, and just laze around and get re-acquainted with one another."

"You don't know how good that sounds Suzanna, but we don't have any extra money now that I'm not working. It takes all Ricky makes for living expenses, and the doctor bills. We never dreamed how expensive having a baby could be. When we don't feel well, we just take the medicine we can get over the counter, but it's different with a baby. You don't know what's wrong with them for sure, so you don't take any chances, you just carry them to their doctor."

"I'll just take some money from my savings, and make you a loan. I will even come over and baby sit for free, while you two are away."

"We can't do that Suzanna."

"Yes you can Janet, when Rick gets home from work, you two decide where you want to go, and how much money you need to borrow."

"Rick won't agree Suzanna, I just know he won't, but it sure sounds tempting to me."

"You just tell Rick that I insist, I need to have a little time with my godchild. Let's see, today is Tuesday, so you have until Friday, to decide how much money you will need. Call me before the bank closes on Friday. I'll pack a bag, and come over for the night, so y'all can get an early start on Saturday morning."

"Oh, this is so exciting. It will be like a honeymoon for us, cries Janet as she hugs me tightly."

"You know Janet, you will have to make a list for me of what to do, and when. If you don't I'll be in big trouble, since I've never been alone with a little one."

Janet could hardly wait for Rick to get home, so they could get started planning their weekend. She fixed an extra good supper, and even made a chocolate cake, Rick's favorite. While Rick was taking his shower, Janet set the table using real linen napkins, and their best dinnerware. Rick finally came in and sat down at the table, when he looked at the food his face lit up with surprise.

"Goodness sweet cakes, what is all this. Did some rich relative die or something? Man this is a feast, you didn't rob a bank did you?" he laughed.

Janet sat down across from him, guess what, I've got great news, Rick. Suzanna is going to make us a loan, and even keep the baby, so we can go somewhere for a weekend alone. Alone Ricky, just you and me, it'll be like a honeymoon."

"Hold on Janet, you know we can't afford a loan from anyone. How would we pay it back, we never have anything extra left from my paycheck?"

"But honey, Suzanna said we can take as long as we need, and pay as little at a time as we can afford. We won't ever get another

40

chance like this, please honey, don't say no."

"I can't deny that it's not tempting and it's been a long time since it was just you and me. Are you sure this won't hurt your friendship with Suzanna? What if you have a falling out about something, and she demands you pay it all back at once?"

"Just trust me Ricky, that will never happen with Suzanna and me."

"It would be great to just get away from everything for a couple of days, and be alone for the first time since "Little Bit's" been in the world," answered Rick.

Janet squealed with delight, and planted kisses all over Rick's face.

"Let's decide where we want to go, and what we want to do, right now, okay honey? I know! We could get the bridal suite in one of the nice hotels, and we could go to the fabulous Fox Theater and see a show. I've never even been to the Fox, have you? We need to call and make reservations right now, and find out how much it will cost, so we will know how much to borrow from Suzanna."

"You are right honey, if we are going first class, we sure don't want to come up short on cash, so you call first thing in the morning and get all the information. There is just one thing I don't agree on, and that's going to the fox." Janet's mouth flew open, ready to protest, but Rick held up his hand and said; Wait until you hear me out before you disagree, okay. I would like to get the bridal suite too, but I would like to just stay in the room and order food when we are hungry, or whatever. It could be like our own little Garden of Eden, and we wouldn't have to see are talk to anyone for two whole days."

"Oh yes, said Janet, that would be so romantic, and it would be like a real honeymoon for sure. "Now that that's all settled, I need to get ready for bed, six o'clock will be here too soon as it is," replied Rick.

Chapter Nine

I decided to drop in to see how Janet had fared in convincing Rick to consider my loan. When she came to the door, I could tell by her sparkling blue eyes that she had won. I followed her back to the kitchen, (our favorite spot) and sat down.

"Rick is going to take you up on that loan for our wild weekend. We've decided to go to Atlanta, and rent the bridal suite in one of the best hotels. We will have all our meals by room service, and well I won't go into detail, you get the picture I'm sure."

"Yes", I laughed, "I'm so glad y'all are going to do this, and I'm also elated that you are going to be close, so if I need you quickly, you will be available."

"Oh my goodness, Suzanna, don't tell me you are afraid to keep "Little Bit," however I can get someone else to keep her, if you'd rather."

"Oh no, Janet, I want to keep her, but if there was an emergency, y'all wouldn't be hours away.

There is one other little thing, I should mention. Bill called and asked me if I would like to go on a picnic Sunday. It will be alright for Jane to go too, won't it?"

"Sure Suzanna, it's fine with me, but does Bill know?"

"Yes, I told him I would be baby-sitting for you, that's when he came up with the picnic idea."

"Wasn't that a thoughtful thing for Bill to suggest? I'm telling you Suzanna that you will never find anyone better. You may not realize it, but I can tell by the way he looks at you that he thinks the world of you." While we were discussing Bill, Janet was packing a bag for "Little Bit", making sure I would have what I needed on our picnic.

"You don't have to do that, Janet, I'll just buy what I need."

"Oh no, I want you to impress Bill, at what an efficient Godmother you are."

"Alright have it your way, Janet, I've got to go now, I have an appointment with Dr. Shannon in about an hour. I wouldn't want to be late on my second time to see him. That might give him the wrong opinion of me."

Doctor Shannon began where we left off last week. "You said you could not recall your childhood, how far back can you remember, Suzanna?"

"I can't remember anything until I became a teen, and as you know that covers only five years of my life. My parents have told me a few things over the years, about my childhood. These things I didn't actually have stored in my memory."

"Have you had anything traumatic happen in your life, which possibly could have blocked your memory?"

"I'm not aware of anything, no one has told me, if I did."

"Right off the top of your head Suzanna, tell me what you are feeling this very minute."

"I feel like I might be dreaming. It's as though I'm standing outside myself, listening to this person talk about me; but I'm really not this person, I don't even know her. She doesn't seem to be a likable person, because she doesn't interest me enough, to want to know her better."

The Doctor sat and looked at me, with a wrinkled brow, then he proceeded to write something on his pad, when he looked up from his writing he still seemed puzzled. Then he asked me, if I would consider letting him hypnotize me on my next visit. I told him I guess it would be okay.

I decided to go by and see Janet on my way home. I wanted to discuss this hypnotizing with her, since I knew nothing about it. Janet reads a lot about medical things, and I'm hoping she knows something about the subject. I told her what the Doctor had said, but Janet was against the idea right away. She told me that sometimes when a person is hypnotized, the hypnotist plants ideas in the patient's mind. She said she would not let anyone hypnotize her, but that I would have to decide for myself. So I guess I will have to think it over before my next visit.

I asked Janet if she had packed for the weekend, she assured me, she had packed at least three times. She said if the day didn't end soon, she was going to have a break down, and she knew she wasn't going to sleep a wink tonight. I told her I would be back about eight, if that would be okay. She said any time at all would be okay, just as long as I didn't forget to come back.

When I drove into the garage, I noticed Mother's car was missing. I wondered where she could be this late in the afternoon. It's not like her at all, to be late getting supper ready for my father.

I went straight to my room to pack my bag for the weekend. I heard Daddy enter the back door. He came to the foot of the stairs, and yelled: "where is everybody?"

"I don't know," I answered on my way down the stairs. When I got home from my appointment with Dr Shannon, Mother wasn't here."

"That's, strange," said Daddy, "your mother never leaves the house without letting me know where she is going."

Then right on cue, we heard Mother pull into the garage. I met her at the back door, ready to defend her if need be. "We were about to get worried about you, Mother." When I looked into her eyes I could see she was upset about something, but I didn't have any inkling why she should be this way. Then Daddy walked into the room all huffy, and demanded to know where she had been, and why she hadn't called to let him know she wouldn't be at home.

To my surprise, Mother snapped at him, telling him they would discuss where she had been later. That right now she had to prepare supper. When Daddy left the room without another word, I almost went into shock.

I asked Mother if she was feeling okay, and her curt reply was," yes I feel fine, why do you ask?"

"I've never heard you use that tone of voice with Daddy before, and you seem upset. Could I help you fix supper?"

Her reply was," no thank you, I'll have it done in a few minutes."

I told her I would finish packing, and be right down to set the table. She gave me a blank look, and asked me where I was going.

"Don't you remember, I told you I would be keeping my godchild for the weekend?"

"Oh yes, I remember you telling me now," but her eyes were so cold, this just wasn't like my mother at all. She hadn't even asked me how my visit went with Doctor Shannon.

I was the only one with anything to say, while we ate supper. You could cut the tension with a knife. When no one was interested in what I had to say, I asked to be excused, so I could get on my way to Janet's.

Chapter Ten

Mary and Frank was finally alone, Frank asked Mary if she was ready to talk about where she had gone today.

"Yes Frank, if you must know I went to see Doctor Shannon, and I had to wait until his last patient left, before he could see me."

"Mary what did you think you would gain in seeing him, you know whatever Suzanna tells him is confidential."

"Yes I know, but I just had to know if he really thought he could help Suzanna. What he told me was scary. He told me he is going to try hypnosis on her next visit."

Mary began to cry. Frank moved over to the couch and placed his arm around Mary's shoulders.

"Honey, I've heard that it's impossible to hypnotize some people, you know Suzanna could be one of those people."

"Even if she can be hypnotized, what is he going to find out? If you ask me, that kind of treatment is highly questionable."

"Oh Frank, I hope you are right. We should have told her everything a long time ago."

"Now you've got to stop worrying about this, Mary. I'll help you with the dishes, and then we can go out to a picture show, how about it?"

"That would be marvelous dear, I can't remember the last time we've been out to a show."

"I know Mary, but Suzanna is a young woman now, with a life of her own. We are going to have to start a new life together, just the two of us. It could be an exciting experience, to bring back the old memories of our youth."

"Frank, do you really think that it is possible, after all these years?"

"I don't see why not," he answered, and he pecked her on the cheek, and then the nose, then the mouth, just the way he used to do, so long ago, it seemed.

When I arrived at Janet's, she had already put the baby down for the night, and Rick was watching a ball game. Janet and I were having a cup of coffee in the kitchen. I told Janet about the episode with Mother and Daddy, and asked her if she thought my mother might be going through menopause. She wanted to know how old Mother was, and I realized I didn't have any idea how old she was. That's when Janet came back with this comment, "good grief Suzanna, I thought everyone knew the age of their parents. You do know her birth date, don't you?"

"Yes her birthday is May sixteenth. You know I always give her a gift, but I've never asked her how old she is, and I've never wondered until now. I hope there is nothing drastically wrong with her, because in all my life I've never heard her be so blunt to my daddy. Do you know the symptoms of menopause?"

"Not really Suzanna, I only know what my aunt told me. She said it could change a woman's personality."

"Oh goodness, I hope that's not what's happening to her. I know Daddy can be a bit over-bearing at times, but I always admired Mother for her patience with him. I know he thinks his way is the only way, but Mother's advice to me has always been that I should just listen to what he says, even if I don't agree. Then I should go on and do what I think is right for me. She's said so many times, Suzanna you know your daddy is like he is, because he loves you, and wants to protect you from all hurt."

"Suzanna, are you telling me that you think this is the first time your parents have had an argument? Surely, it was just the first time they've disagreed in your presence. You are always saying that they overprotect you. Maybe they think you are old enough to know now that life isn't always a bed of roses, and that no two people always have the same point of view, on all subjects that's for sure. Don't go looking for something to worry about, just let life happen. You take everything too seriously, for goodness' sake, lighten up."

"Thank you Janet, I feel better now that I've talked with you. If you don't mind I believe I'll go to bed now. It's been a long and trying day."

Chapter Eleven

The next morning Janet and Rick left real early for their fun weekend. "Little Bit" and I were sitting in the middle of the living room floor, with books scattered all around us, when the doorbell rang. I couldn't imagine who it could be so early in the morning. When I opened the door, there stood Bill. What a great surprise I thought, but why is he here?

"Come on in Bill, we are just reading some of "Little Bit's" books, it's nice to see you."

"I hope you don't mind me dropping in without calling first."

"Oh no," I answered. "Would you like a cup of coffee?"

"No thanks, I know it's early, but it's such a beautiful day, I thought we might get an early start to the park," he replied.

"That's, a great idea, but I thought you said we were going to the park on Sunday."

"I did, but why waste a sunny day like today, it might be raining tomorrow. I'm looking forward to seeing the baby's reaction to all those animals. I think she will enjoy Grants Park, don't you?"

"Oh my yes, and I will too, I can't remember how many years it's been, since I've been to the park. Just give me a minute to get "Little Bit's bag." I picked up the bag and hurried back to the living room, all the while hoping this would be a fun day, for all of us. Bill had taken baby Jane in his arms, and it was amazing to me how natural he looked holding the child.

I hope we won't have any problems with "Little Bit." I want so much to show Bill that I am good with children. Maybe he won't notice how nervous I am. Little kids scare me, for I've never even been around a small child before. Bill seems so relaxed and comfortable with "Little Bit". The petting zoo was her favorite, because she could touch the goats and sheep. It was a bright sunny day, and so rewarding, to see Jane's big blue eyes light up, as we strolled from pen to pen. We told her the name of each animal, and she would repeat after us, and giggle with joy.

When we finally got back home, I was exhausted Bill helped me with "Little Bit's" bath, then we fed her, and she was nodding before she finished eating. We tucked her in bed, and quietly slipped out to the living room.

"Goodness Bill, I had no idea how demanding it could be, to care for a baby full time. I feel sorry for Janet, she has every day like this."

"It's not as tiring for Janet, because she has had time to get used to the routine," said Bill.

"Let's see what's on TV we might find a good movie."

"That sounds good to me," Bill answered.

There was a movie on, but it was a western, and I fell asleep. Needless to say when I awoke I was so humiliated. "I'm so sorry Bill why didn't you wake me?"

"There's nothing to apologize for, you were just tired and needed a little nap. After all you are not used to little ones. It's two o'clock, if we are going on another picnic tomorrow, I'd better head for home," It was so late I couldn't see Bill having to go home, and come right back tomorrow, so I invited him to spend the night. I found him a pair of Rick's pajamas, and made up the couch, while he took a shower. During that time I had time to think about what I had done. I started to worry that Bill would get the wrong impression of me, or my morals anyway. When he came back from his shower, he ask me if I were sure it would be okay for him to stay the night. I assured him it was okay, and excused myself right away, heading for the bedroom. I lay awake for a long time, wondering if my decision was a wise one. To tell the truth, I felt safe with Bill here, because if something should happen to "Little Bit"; he would know what to do. Let's face it; he knows lots more about babies than I do. "Little Bit" seems to sense this also, she adores Bill, and quiet frankly she prefers him to me.

When I awoke the next morning, I dressed and my intention was to quietly fix breakfast. I walked into the kitchen and found Bill feeding "Little Bit" her meal. I asked him why he hadn't called me. He said when he looked in on me that I was sleeping so peacefully he didn't have the heart to disturb me. He's going to make someone a wonderful husband.

Today we took little Jane Marie to Stone Mountain Park. We

rode the train, and she giggled the whole trip. We ended up taking the second train ride before we could interest her in anything else. It amazed me how much Bill seemed to enjoy being with us. Being in charge of a child doesn't bother him in the least. I can't imagine me being alone with "Little Bit" for the whole weekend. Bill doesn't know how valuable he has been to me. I might as well admit it; I'm just not mother material.

When we got back to the apartment, Janet and Rick were home. They were thrilled to be with their baby again, and Janet was glowing with happiness. No one had to ask them how their weekend had been it was written all over their faces. Bill and I didn't tarry long, for we knew they needed to be alone, to settle down with "Little Bit." I dreaded the parting with Bill; this weekend had been the happiest time in my life.

I guess he didn't want to say good-bye any more than I did, because he asked me if I would like to have a bite to eat. I said sure, although I wasn't the least bit hungry. On my way home after leaving the restaurant, I pondered on what Janet had been saying about marriage. When and if I do settle down someday, I would surely want my husband to be as thoughtful as Bill. I couldn't help myself, I wondered if Bill was being himself, or was he just trying to impress me.

When I arrived home, Mother was in the kitchen as usual, so I pulled out a stool and sat at the counter watching her every movement. She doesn't look any older, but I can sense something is just not right in her life at this time.

She looked up from her salad fixing, "How was your baby sitting dear? I expected you to call me at least once."

Oh, Mother, I had a wonderful weekend; Bill took us to Grant's Park on Saturday, and to Stone Mountain today. He was my lifesaver helping care for little Jane Marie. He knows all there is to know, about little ones."

Mother pursed her lips and placed one hand beneath her chin as she replied, "I don't remember you telling me that your friend Bill has children, are you sure he's not married?"

"Good Grief! Mother, Bill's not married and never has been, and he surely doesn't have any kids of his own. It's just that he has seven brothers and sisters, all younger than him." I suddenly realized this conversation gave me an opening to ask some questions of my own.

"Mother, why didn't you have more children? Was I such a bad little girl that you couldn't face having any more? How old were you when I was born?"

Mother seemed shaken with all my questions. I saw the wrinkle come in her brow that she uses to tell me she has had enough questions from me. But then to my surprise she started to answer.

"Let's see you were born in 1936, and your daddy and I had been married four years. I was twenty-four when I wed your father, so that would have made me twenty-eight when you were born. Why after all these years do you ask such questions dear?"

"Well Mother, I couldn't believe what happened between you and Daddy last Friday evening.

The more I thought about it the more I wondered if you could be going through menopause. I realized I didn't even know how old you are, so that's why I am asking these questions."

"You know honey you could be absolutely right, why it hadn't crossed my mind. I will have to make an appointment with Doctor Browne. Now would you help me get the food on the table, please."

Chapter Twelve

I was up early the next morning. I couldn't wait to hear about Janet's weekend. I rang her bell the third time, before she answered.

"Suzanna I couldn't imagine who was here so early! Goodness, come on in."

I apologized and told her I could come back later. "I wanted to hear all about your weekend and tell you about mine, but it can wait until another time if you are busy."

"Don't be silly," she answered, "come on in the kitchen and I'll brew us a pot of coffee, and we will talk all day if you want to. So let's see now, where do we begin?" I told her that I wanted to hear about her, and I didn't want her to leave out anything, using her favorite phrase. It didn't take any coaxing to get Janet started, she was dying to talk about her weekend, just as I was eager to talk about mine.

"Oh, Suzanna, it was so romantic, just like I had always dreamed my honeymoon would be. I think Rick and I can say we truly know each other now. We talked more than we did the whole time we were dating. I had forgotten how lucky I am to have him; in fact I think we both were at the point of taking each other for granted. I will always be indebted to you for seeing our need to get away, and to just spend all our time with each other. But enough about us, I want to hear about you now, Suzanna."

"Janet it was marvelous, I still can't get over how much Bill knows about children. "Little Bit" is just crazy about him. He stayed over Saturday night, and he was up feeding your child when I finally woke up, then he insisted on helping do the dishes." Janet held her hand out like a traffic cop saying, "Wait, wait a minute, did I hear you say that Bill spent the night here?" She had this sly smile on her face, like the cat that ate the canary. I rushed on to tell her it wasn't what she was thinking. I told her, Bill being the gentleman he was slept on the couch. "I let him wear a pair of Rick's pajamas, I didn't think you would mind."

"No problem, friend, but I don't know if I believe you about him sleeping on the couch. What's wrong with you Suzanna, ain't you attracted just a little bit to that good looking man?"

"If you want the truth Janet, Bill makes my heart sing. I went to sleep (by myself in your bed) contemplating on the fact that it wouldn't be half bad to spend the rest of my life with someone like Bill. Janet, I had the happiest time of my life this past weekend."

"Oh, Suzanna, this is just wonderful news."

"Just wait one minute Janet, don't get overly excited, I have no idea if Bill feels the same way about me. After all we don't go out that often you know."

"Good Gracious, Suzanna, you've got to show some emotions, when you are with Bill. If you don't, how do you think he will ever know how you feel about him?"

"I've given it a lot of serious thought actually, and I've decided I will wait until I'm dismissed from Doctor Shannon's care, before I get too close to Bill. He is just too good a person; I would never want to hurt him. By the way, I need to discuss something concerning my next appointment with Doctor Shannon. Do you know anything about hypnosis? The doctor asked me would I agree to hypnosis on my next visit. I nonchalantly said okay, without asking any details. Now I'm having second thoughts. Somehow it just doesn't feel right, but it might be because I don't know enough about the technique. What would you do if it were you Janet?"

"I only know what I've read about it Suzanna, but I'm not sure I would agree to be hypnotized.

I've read that the person who does the hypnotizing, can plant thoughts in you mind, and that is frightening to me. You would need complete confidence in your doctor for sure."

"I think I'll tell him I want to wait a while longer, to see if I can get better by just talking to him."

Today I have an appointment for my next session with Doctor Shannon. I wish I could be sure that this therapy is going to solve my problems. But like my father says nothing is sure, but death and taxes.

I'm feeling better since I started my visits, but I don't know if it's the therapy or meeting Bill that's making things worth while for me. This is the first time I've had to wait to See Doctor Shannon. The receptionist came to the door and called my name. When I entered the Office Doctor Shannon extended his hand, and asked me to have a seat.

"Let's see now," he said, as he looked at his notes from last week, here we are, as he flipped through the pages, we are going to use hypnosis today. Are you ready to get started Suzanna?"

"I'm feeling much better now, and I really don't think I need to go into hypnosis, not at this time."

"Well it's completely up to you, Suzanna, so what do you want to talk about today?"

"I've met this wonderful person, and I think he may eventually ask me to marry him. I was wondering if you think I should tell him I'm under your care? I know in my heart, he has a right to know I have an emotional problem, but I'm afraid it might scare him away.

You know what people think if a person is seeing a psychiatrist, that they are crazy. How can I explain to him why I need your help? Would it be so wrong if I don't tell him? I don't intend to get married to anyone, until I am a whole person."

"You know Suzanna, what you and I talk about is strictly confidential. If you plan to be okay, before you commit yourself to marriage, then there is no problem. You are a wise and mature person to feel this way, and I'm sure you will be a more stable person when I dismiss you."

"Thanks Doctor, that's a load off my mind. Later on if you decide that I should go under hypnosis then I will do it. I know I can trust your judgment, or Doctor Browne would not have recommended you."

Bill calls me almost every evening, and I just know he is my soul mate. I wish I could be sure he feels the same way. I've given a lot of thought on how to approach Mother and Daddy, and there isn't any easy way to do it. I'm gonna tell them at supper tonight. Well needless to say, I chickened out while we were eating. When I was helping clear away the table, I asked Mother if I could ask Bill over for Sunday dinner. I told her I wanted her and Daddy to meet Bill. She assured me it would be fine, that they would like to get to know Bill. She also told me that she couldn't help but notice that Bill and I were seeing an awful lot of each other to just be friends.

I knew I was opening a can of worms, but that's when I told Mother I was in love with Bill. "Oh goodness, Suzanna, she replied, you promised to go to college for at least two years.

You have plenty of time to fall in love, but you will be young only once. You are not old enough to take the responsibilities of marriage and family. This Bill can't possibly give you the life style you have had all your life. When you have children, you will need help with them. Right now I know you think love is all that matters, but you can't live on love alone. Just look at your friend Janet, they live from payday to payday, just think how dull your life would be, if you had to live like that. Bill didn't go to college, and you and I know he will never make a lot of money. Honey, I want more for you than he can give you, you deserve more."

"Why Mother I never knew you felt the same as Daddy, about money and material things. Janet and Rick are very much in love, and completely happy with their life. They love their daughter as much as you love me."

"I never implied that Janet doesn't love her child, but how will they ever give her security, Suzanna."

"Love is security," I shouted and ran for the back door, to escape any more hurting words.

Mary was upset and she headed for the study, where she knew she would find Frank and his paper. "Frank, turn the TV off please, we need to talk."

"What's all the noise about, did I hear the back door slam."

"You certainly did, it was Suzanna leaving in a huff. We have a problem, Suzanna is thinking about getting married. We have just got to find a way to stop her Frank. She told me she is in love with Bill, and frankly I don't believe she knows what love is," cried Mary, her voice getting more and more shrill

"Now get hold of yourself, Mary, you know there is nothing we can do to stop her, she is of age."

"That's true, but Frank that boy doesn't make enough money to get married. We don't know anything about him or his family. Suzanna is not well enough emotionally to cope with her life right now, much less make a life with someone else. She certainly isn't ready to have a family, to have a baby right now, would probably push her right over the edge."

"Mary you have to face reality, we can't live Suzanna's life for her. We have our lives to think about. I think maybe it's time to let her go."

"FRANK! What are you saying? I always felt you didn't love her as much as I do, but I thought you cared more than this".

"Honey, you know I love Suzanna as much as you do, but we can't protect her from herself."

"I never thought of you as a quitter Frank, you might give up, but I never will. I'm going to call Doctor Shannon tomorrow, and ask him to do something to change her mind."

"Just what do you think the Doctor can do. Would you want him to lock her away in a mental hospital for the rest of her life, that's about all he could do."

"No, you know I don't want anything of the kind. I do think he might know how to discourage her. If anyone can make her see she's not ready for marriage, surely he can, after all he is a professional."

"Mary, dear Mary, go ahead and call her Doctor, if it will make you feel better, but don't expect a miracle. You know as well as I that once Suzanna sets her mind to something, no one can change it, but no one."

"I'll admit she is stubborn, but I can't just sit and do nothing, while she ruins her life."

Chapter Thirteen

When I rushed out of the house, I had no idea where I would go. I finally ended up at Janet's door.

"Janet I'm sorry to bother you while Rick is home, but I just have to talk to someone." I couldn't hold back my tears any longer; I was actually close to hysteria.

"That's perfectly all right, Rick is watching TV in our bedroom. You know I'm here anytime you need me, what are friends for. Come on into the kitchen, and I'll make us something to drink." Janet fixed our drinks and sat down across from me.

"Now then, tell me what's so terrible; it's not Bill I hope."

"I hate my parents. I tried to talk to Mother about the way I feel about Bill. She acted like I had lost my mind, when I told her I thought I loved him. She went on and on about this stuff, about me not being old enough to even think about love, let alone marriage. What it boils down to is she doesn't think Bill is good enough for her princess. He doesn't have a college education like Daddy, so he will never be successful. I didn't know until now that Mother thinks just like Daddy. Money and material things is all they think about. Mother simply can't love me, and not want me to be happy, and I know Daddy will uphold her against me."

"Now Suzanna I know your parents love you, and you do too. They just don't know what a great guy Bill is, since they have never met him."

I can't say for sure they would change their minds if they did know him, but you should give them a fair chance. They just don't want you to have to sacrifice, and I can understand that. To them money and status are security, and they want to know that you will always be secure."

"Janet you of all people know that money doesn't buy happiness."

"Yes Suzanna, you and I know that, but undoubtedly your parents don't see things that way. They are just lucky to have money and love."

"When and if I should have a daughter, I will want her happiness, above anything else in her life. It won't matter if the man she falls in love with, doesn't have a dime."

"Okay Suzanna, I think if you will give your parents a chance, they'll come around. Invite Bill over and let them get to know him. I don't think it will be easy to fault him, once they meet him."

"Janet, you just don't know my parents. Sure you've been in my house, often over the years, but you never saw the true side of them. The last thing my mother said, before I stormed out of the house, was that she didn't want me to have to live like my friend Janet. It's her judgment that you can never give your daughter the things she deserves."

"Did your mother really say that Suzanna? You know I never thought of your mother as a snob. She surely had me fooled."

"I'll tell you one thing though, Janet, if Bill ask me to marry him we will elope. I will wash my hands of my parents, and never ask them for another thing."

"But Bill hasn't asked you to marry him. You are just angry, and upset right now. In your frame of mind it's not possible for you to decide anything."

"I know you are probably right, but I also know that my parents will never give Bill a warm welcome into the family. Bill is going to ask me to marry him, just wait and see."

"When he does I'm gonna say yes, even if it means my parents will disown me."

"For right now Suzanna, try to get along with your folks. Just don't bring up the word marriage anymore. You need to go on back home now, and apologize."

"I thought I might spend the night here, and let them wonder where I am."

"That's not a good idea, you know you are under a Doctor's care, and your parents would be frantic. So don't upset them any more than you have already, and Suzanna if they ask where you have been, tell them you have been driving around thinking, and that you are sorry for your outburst."

Janet walked me to the door, and asked me to call her later to let her know how things were going. While driving home, I couldn't help but think that Janet was siding with my parents.

A year ago she would have agreed with me wholeheartedly. It seemed since she became a mother herself she had changed a lot. I might as well face the fact that being married has changed Janet; we will never be as close as we were before she married. She has her own happy little world now.

When I arrived home, I found Mother and Daddy in the study. Mother looked up from her book. I dropped down on my knees in front of her chair. It was hard to keep from crying, as our eyes met.

"Where have you been Suzanna, over at your friend Janet's no doubt?"

"Mother I'm sorry I lost my temper. I've been driving around and thinking, and I realize you are absolutely right. I know I'm not ready for marriage yet, however, I still would like for you, and Daddy to meet Bill. He's really a good person, and I believe y'all would like him, once you get to know him."

"Why certainly honey, you can invite him for Sunday dinner, you know your friends are always welcome in our home."

"Please promise me if and when he comes you won't embarrass him; he's a very sensitive person."

"Now why on earth do you think that Suzanna? How could I embarrass him? I cannot understand where you get such ideas?"

I felt myself getting ready to flare up, at this remark from Mother. I caught myself in time thank goodness, and I arose from my knees smiling at her.

"I'm tired, I think I'll go up to bed now Mother, goodnight."

The next day I visited Janet to let her know how things went.

"You did good, said Janet; I couldn't have done any better myself."

"You can say I'm learning, thanks to you Janet. From now on I'm going to say what Mother wants to hear. I'm going to invite Bill over on Sunday, and see what happens."

"Just don't be on the defensive when you talk to your mother about Bill."

"I know you are right, but she can be so critical of people. If she and Daddy start the third degree with Bill, I will just walk out with him, even if it's in the middle of the meal. They are simply not gonna humiliate him in my presence, that's how strongly I feel about him."

"I know my friend," answered Janet," just don't rock the boat, for your own sake."

Bill and I were at the drive-in when I decided to ask him to come to Dinner on Sunday.

"I don't know, Suzanna, I wouldn't know what to talk about with your folks."

I asked him why he never has any trouble talking to me. Even on our first date, it was as though we were old friends. "My parents are just ordinary people. You can talk to them about anything that comes to mind." I was surprised to hear his answer.

"Suzanna, your home is a mansion compared to my home. You probably could put our whole house in your living room. Anyone can see that your parents have money, and kids are all my folks have. I didn't know all this the first time I met you, I would have been completely tongue-tied if I had known."

"I've already made plans with Mother and Daddy for you to meet them, you've just gotta come Sunday."

"Okay, but I might be an embarrassment to you, before the evening is over."

"Nonsense, you won't embarrass me no matter what happens. You just relax, and be yourself, and my folks will like you almost as much as I do."

Sunday arrived and Bill was almost sick with anxiety, why he wondered did I agree to this meeting with Suzanna's parents. He rang the bell with damp palms. Mr. Stoggins opened the door. I heard Daddy ask Bill to come in. When they entered the living room, my mother extended her hand. "I feel we already know you Bill," she said. I realized I had been standing there holding my breath the whole time. To my dismay Mother had asked Aunt Mattie, (the old black lady that had been in the family all my life practically) to come over and serve our meal. That's just like Mother to show-off; she knew that Bill didn't have servants in his home. I think she only did this to make Bill uncomfortable. I looked at Bill across the table from me, and I could see he was nervous; he could hardly keep from choking. The questions my parents were asking were almost as if he were on trial. I kept trying to rescue him, but to no avail.

When the meal was finally over I asked to be excused to freshen up, so we wouldn't be late for our next engagement, which did not exist, I knew I had to get Bill out of there. When we were in the car, I apologized to Bill. I explained to him if I had know they were going to give him the third degree, I would have never invited him. I told him Mother had promised me, they would not get personal with their questions.

His reply was that he didn't blame them. If he were in their shoes he probably would have done the same. I tried to explain to him that just because they might not approve of him, didn't mean that I could not choose him. He explained to me that he knew he could never fit into my family.

I came back with the fact that I was in love with him, even if he could never fit into my family.

"This can't be Suzanna," he said, "your folks would never allow you to marry someone like me. I would never be able to give you the kind of life you are accustom to. I realize that I will never be rich."

"You are rich in kindness, and love and understanding, and those are the things I need. They are the things that are missing in my life, Bill. My parents can't buy these things for me, but you have them all to give to me. Don't you see, that makes you richer than my folks will ever be."

Bill pulled the car to the side of the road and stopped, he turned and gently drew me into his arms. What followed just seemed natural. I had never felt so loved before. I also knew I would not want to live without Bill. I thought I was in love with Fred, now I know real love. I didn't feel any guilt or shame for making love with Bill. There was no doubt in my mind that Bill was my true soul mate.

Bill was upset about what had happened.

"Suzanna, I'm so sorry, I don't know what came over me. I've never done anything like this before. I hope you don't think I planned it, you've got to believe me, I swear I didn't"

"Shhhhhh, I whispered, I'm not sorry, and I know you didn't plan it."

"What if you get pregnant, we didn't use any protection," Bill asked.

61

"So what," I answered, "we will be getting married now anyway."

"Suzanna I wouldn't want anyone to think we had to get married."

"It doesn't matter what people think, if I am pregnant, my parents would have to agree for us to be married."

"You don't know that for sure, they could send you away to have it, and make you put it up for adoption "

"You are forgetting one thing Bill, I am of age to do as I please now and no one can make me give up anything."

"The thing is Suzanna, I'm not ready to get married, and I don't think you are either. I want to save enough money to buy our own home before we talk about marriage, and we surely don't need a baby right away."

"I'm beginning to understand, why don't you just come out and say that you don't love me."

"I do love you Suzanna, more than anything else in the world, and when the time is right I want you to be my wife. You don't understand, because you have lived a sheltered life. I know how hard it is to have a family, and no home of your own. That is my background and I don't want you to ever be exposed to that kind of stress. I want to be able to take good care of you, and I want you to be proud to call me your husband."

"Bill you are the most wonderful person I've ever known, I'm proud of you this moment. You sound just like Mother and Daddy right now. Let me be the one to say what I want and need...

All I want is to be a normal person, with an average life, with the one I love. I know we can't have everything at first, I'm well aware that we will have to build a life together, one step at a time."

"Suzanna, that's all right, but I need time to get used to the idea of marriage. Remember when we first met, you were the one who said you were not ready for a commitment. It was your idea to be just friends, and I agreed."

"Oh I see, I was wrong about you, Bill Norton. You are just like all the other men in the world. Once you get what you want, you are ready to move on to your next victim. Well don't you worry about me if I'm pregnant, I can take care of myself. Now take me home.

Men! You are all alike, I don't need any of you anymore,"

We drove to my home in complete silence. Once his car stopped in the drive I jumped out, and ran for the porch. I ran up the stairs into my room and fell across my bed, crying my heart out. All I could think was there had to be something terribly wrong with me. It seemed no one could love me. What will I do if I did get pregnant tonight? Bill's probably right my parents would send me away, they would not tolerate a scandal.

I got up from my bed and went into my bathroom. I have no desire to live anymore.

I look at my reflection in the mirror I'm not a beauty queen, but I'm not an ugly duckling either.

My hair is naturally curly and it's auburn in color. My eyes are almost black. I'm of average height. My weight is one hundred twenty pounds. I am cursed with the inner voice that no one wants to hear about. I don't see but one way to eliminate the voice. I lock the bathroom door and pick up the razor, but I don't want to make a mess for Mother to have to clean up. I stepped over into the tub, and sat down. I look ahead while I cut my left wrist, it didn't hurt nearly as much as I thought it might. I take the blade in my left hand, and cut my right wrist. I sit here wondering how long it will take. Now I feel as though I'm fading into the night, not a bad feeling really.

Bill had never felt so badly before in his life. He had never taken advantage of any other girl he had dated. He was a virgin until tonight, but then he had never been in love before either. Of all the people to hurt, why did it have to be Suzanna? There was no doubt about it; he knew he was in love with her. He also knew he simply wasn't financially able to get married at this time.

He was still helping his folks make ends meet. This was something he knew Suzanna would never understand.

He knew someone like Suzanna would find another worthier of her. He also knew he would never love another the way he loved her. He would never call her again. She must hate him now. Suzanna would have to call him, if she could ever forgive him for what happened. He was too ashamed to ask her for forgiveness.

Mary heard Suzanna run up the stairs, and somehow she felt that something was not right. She waited listening, and thinking Suzanna might come to her door. After a few seconds she realized from her gut feeling that something was wrong. The feeling was not going to subside. She reached for her robe and stepped across the hall to Suzanna door. She knocked and called her daughter's name. There was no sound from the room. She turned the knob and the door opened. She stepped inside, but as she looked around, she realized Suzanna was in the bathroom.

She walked over to the door, and put her ear close. But she didn't hear a sound. She tried the knob, and found the door locked. She called to Suzanna, and asked her if she was okay, but there was only silence. She was becoming frightened, so she screamed for Suzanna to open the door. She could feel the tightness of fear. It was like a steel band around her chest. Frank came running, "what is wrong with you Mary, don't you know it's the middle of the night?"

"I don't know for sure what is wrong," Mary screamed, "please see if you can force the door open and hurry!"

Frank put his shoulder to the door, but he knew he couldn't do it that way. He was not a strong person physically. He picked up a chair and slammed it against the lock, but this only broke the legs off the chair. Mary ran for the phone, and dialed the police,

When the policemen arrived, they forced the door open, and Mary rushed in, only to pass out from the sight. Suzanna was lying unconscious in the tub, fully clothed. Both wrist were freely bleeding from the razor cuts. Frank was trying to bring Mary out of her faint, and all he could say was why, why, why. The ambulance arrived and took Suzanna to the nearest hospital. Mary and Frank followed in the car. Neither of them spoke for a long time it seemed, and then Mary began to cry.

"Please don't cry honey," said Frank, "She's gonna be alright, she just has to."

"It's our fault you know; we should have told her the truth a long time ago. We have been living a lie all these years. And when she started going to see Dr. Shannon, we should have known something like this could happen," cried Mary.

"I don't agree, I don't think it would have mattered at all even if she knew everything. Suzanna always has had a self-destructive nature. It's something I have never understood, but I don't blame you, or me for what she has done tonight," answered Frank.

"Well I can't live like this anymore, if she pulls through I will tell her everything," was Mary's answer.

Chapter Fourteen

When I awoke I was in a strange room, it didn't take me long to realize it was a hospital room. I couldn't for the life of me imagine why I was here. I didn't feel any pain, I couldn't remember being sick, and I couldn't remember coming here. I looked toward the door, I saw my mother entering, and her first words were, "Oh thank goodness, you have finally come out of the coma."

"How do you feel, honey?"

"What happened, and why have I been in a coma?"

Mother had a blank look on her face, when she finally found her voice she said, "Wait just a moment dear, and I'll go get a nurse," and she hurried out of the room.

Mary ran to the nurses' station, "Suzanna is awake, and I need someone to come with me to her room."

"Sure answered one of the nurses, you could have just turned the light on ma'am, there wasn't any need for you to have to leave her alone."

"No, you don't understand," answered Mary, "Suzanna doesn't even know why she's here. It's as though she has no idea what happened. I didn't know what to tell her."

"Oh," said the nurse, "maybe I should call Dr. Shannon to come in to see her. I don't know if it would be wise to tell her what happened, since she doesn't remember."

"You should go back to her room. She might be afraid to be alone, just make light conversation until I can get the Doctor to come in, or at least ask him what we should do."

I lay there trying to make some kind of sense to my delirium, but I just kept coming up with one big blank. I wish Mother would come back and answer some questions. I need to know why I'm here most of all. I looked toward the door, and Mother was just coming back in.

"I'm so glad you are back Mother, now maybe you can tell me why in this world have I been in a coma? How long have I been here? "What caused the coma?

"Well honey, you had an accident. When we found you, you were unconscious. I'm sure that's why you don't remember anything."

"What kind of accident Mother?"

"Your daddy and I found you in the bathtub," Mother said in a whisper, as if she hoped no one else would hear.

Tears of anger and frustration ran down my face, as my memory came back.

"Oh, Mother, now I remember and you know it wasn't an accident as well as I do. I tried to kill myself why didn't you let me die?" At that moment Dr. Shannon walked into my room, and Mother ran from the room, sobbing as though her heart was breaking.

"Welcome back into the world Suzanna," was Dr. Shannon's first words. "How are you feeling?"

"I'm not sure I want to be back, why didn't you let me die? It's my life and should be my decision to live or die."

"With that kind of answer I can tell you, you are going to need a lot of help. Believe me, you are going to get well, I promise you that. Now talk to me, the sooner we start the better," said Doctor Shannon.

"I really don't think all the talk in the world is going to make a difference. I don't believe I will ever be well. Something is missing inside. I think Mother probably knows. The part I don't understand is why for some strange reason she doesn't want me to know. Why would my own mother not want me to get well?"

"Okay, Suzanna, I'll have a talk with your mother. On one condition though, you have to promise me you won't try to harm yourself anymore, okay?"

"Only if you will promise me that I will get well for sure, without a doubt."

"I can promise you I won't leave one stone unturned, and I will do everything in my power to help you get well, Suzanna. I will phone your mother tonight and make an appointment to talk with her. At present I want you to get lots of sleep, can you do that for me?"

"That won't be a problem, there is nothing else to do here," I answered.

When Frank reached home from his office, he found Mary crying, and more distraught than ever.

"What happened, Suzanna isn't worse is she?" he asked.

"No she's back with us, but I'm not sure she will ever get any better. We've just got to talk to her she has the right to know, Frank."

"Sure honey, but don't you think that we should talk it over with Dr. Shannon first, to make sure it's the right thing, and the right time?"

"Well yes, I suppose you have a point, dear," answered Mary.

The phone rang. Mary picked up; and like a blessing from above, it was Dr. Shannon on the other end.

"Hello," said Mary, Dr. Shannon I was just about to call you, and make an appointment for tomorrow morning. Do you think you could see me that soon?"

"I was hoping maybe you and your husband could make time for me, to come over this evening, we really do need to talk, as soon as possible," said the Doctor.

"Yes, you certainly may come over, would around eight be okay for you, if not you give the hour best for you."

"Thank you, Mrs. Stoggins, eight will be fine."

Mary turned to her husband. "Can you believe it, that was Dr. Shannon, he's coming here around eight to talk with us."

"Okay, Mary, let's get together on this, before he arrives. We need to determine how much, and what we want to tell him."

"Frank! Just listen to yourself we are going to have to tell him everything. If we want him to help Suzanna, we can't hold back anything!" exclaimed Mary.

Dr. Shannon arrived promptly at eight. "Would you like a drink, asked Frank, extending his hand to the doctor.

"No thank you, I'm on call at the hospital tonight, so we need to get started right away. We could be interrupted at any time, so every minute counts."

After that comment everyone took a seat. Mary sat on the edge of her easy chair, holding her hands tightly, with a painful look in her eyes. She took a long breath and began, as though it took every bit of strength she had.

"The fact is that we aren't Suzanna's biological parents. We got her through a private adoption when she was only an hour old.

"I've always felt that she senses she isn't ours, but she has never come right out and asked."

"When you say private, what exactly does that entail?" asked Dr. Shannon.

"We gave the Doctor the money for the care of the mother. When the baby was born, we were called to the clinic to pick her up. The Doctor didn't offer any information about the Mother at the time, and we were so excited, we didn't ask any questions. Dr. Wallace told us the mother couldn't take care of the baby properly. We never asked her name, or even where she lived. Dr. Wallace arranged for the birth certificate to state our name as the parents. Suzanna didn't spend any time in the clinic, the Doctor made house calls to make sure she was doing okay. He never explained to us, what he told the nurse who helped with the delivery. I personally think maybe he told her the baby died. I was just so happy to have a baby to call my own, I didn't care to know all the details, at the time. For years I worried that the mother might come looking for her, but as the years went by, I assumed she really never wanted her baby. Since there was no way for anyone to know the truth, we decided to never tell Suzanna. But I won't deny that Suzanna has always sensed something was missing, from the time she was a small child. Please tell us what to do Dr. Shannon we love her as if she were our own. We are afraid she will never forgive us, if we tell her the truth now we know we should have told her long ago, but we just never could find the right time. At least that's what we kept telling ourselves. We won't you to decide when it will be the right time to tell her."

Doctor Shannon could hardly believe the words he was hearing. In all his years of practice, he had never heard anything to compare to this confession. He would have to give this some serious thought. Dr. Shannon got up from his seat hurriedly I must go, I need to be alone to think, and try to absorb what you have told me."

"You do think Suzanna will get a lot better if she knows the truth, don't you?" said Mary.

"Frankly, I'm not sure what this might do to Suzanna. It's a shock to me even in my profession."

After the Doctor had left, Mary broke completely; she could hardly climb the stairs to their bedroom. She crawled into bed fully dressed, and drew her knees into a fetal position. Her last thought before she drifted into sleep was, beware for your sins will find you out. She had heard her dear Mother say those words so many times, when she was just a little girl. Until now it had never registered with her. She felt so lost and alone. Why was the good deed they did, turning into such an ugly secret? How could it be so wrong to love a child that she didn't carry in her own body? The woman that did carry Suzanna didn't love her enough to keep her, wasn't that a greater sin?

Dr. Shannon left the Stoggins' home with a bigger problem than he had before the meeting. For the facts were so upsetting to him, he felt he could not tell Suzanna. He had to talk to Suzanna, and try to find a way to help her. He felt it would do her more harm, than good in her present state of mind. He had never had so much compassion for any patient before. He could almost feel her pain, she was a warm and caring person, but she was still holding her guard up.

He knew she was keeping things of importance from him in their meetings, he didn't know if he would ever have her complete trust. Somehow he doubted it. If he had had a daughter, he wouldn't have been any more concerned about her well being. Somehow Suzanna had found a niche in his heart, and he felt he just had to find an escape for her.

I was lying in bed looking out on the hospital grounds, completely bored, when Dr. Shannon came by to see me. He came over to my bedside and covered my hand with his own. He smiled and asked me how I was feeling. I told him I felt okay, and then I asked him if he had spoken to Mother. He told me he had talked with my parents, but they didn't have any answers. He told me he was going to move me to the fourth floor for a few days. Just to give me some added rest, until we decided what treatment would be best for me. I knew the fourth floor is the psychiatric ward, and I told him I didn't feel that I belonged on that floor. He explained that I would need some counseling before he could dismiss me.

Chapter Fifteen

It's been two weeks now, and here I sit looking out the hospital window. I don't know how long Dr. Shannon plans to keep me here. He promised he would find some answers for me, but I'm beginning to feel like a prisoner of this hospital.

"Penny for your thoughts," I hear from the door behind me. I turned to look and it is Dr. Shannon. He smiled and asked, "How is my favorite patient today?"

"How would you feel, if you were in here, and didn't have any idea when you would get out?"

"Now Suzanna, you know we are doing our best to help you. Don't you feel just a little bit better?"

"I don't see why you think I can feel any differently. You can't explain what is wrong with me, have you decided to just keep me here indefinitely, or are you waiting for me to tell you I am well, so you don't have the responsibility for me anymore? How long do you plan to keep me here against my will, or do you have any idea?"

"I'm sorry you feel this way, however I do have to try to keep you from harming yourself again."

"Okay I won't harm myself anymore, now can I go home?"

"Suzanna, there is one other treatment that might help you, however it is risky, and you would have to sign a release that if something goes wrong the hospital won't be held accountable."

"What is this treatment?"

"Shock Therapy; an electric shock is applied to the brain. It's only harmful if you should have an aneurysm in the brain. We will do a brain scan to rule out such weakness, before we give the first treatment. You will be asleep for the treatment, therefore you won't feel anything."

"What is an aneurysm, Dr. Shannon?"

"It's a sac, formed by local enlargement of the weakened wall of an artery. This is why we have to have your signed consent to do this procedure. The first treatment could be fatal, if we should fail to detect an aneurysm."

"What is this treatment supposed to do to help me?"

"It will rearrange your brain waves, and hopefully erase the bad vibes your subconscious is holding. It will also erase some of your short-term memory, and you will feel lost for a while afterwards."

"Will I have to have more than one of these treatments?"

"Yes, there will be more than one, but I couldn't tell you the exact number it will take. You will get a treatment every other day. On the day of treatment, you may not even remember your name, but that will only be temporary. I can't promise you that this will make everything the way you want it to be, but it's all I have to offer at this time. I can't tell you how much of your memory you may lose, or how much you will regain. You might want to talk this over with you parents, before you decide, it is a big decision."

"No Dr. Shannon, I don't need to talk it over with anyone; I know I want to do this. As far as memory goes, as you know, I don't have that much to lose. Do you think we could start the treatment tomorrow, the sooner the better with me."

"Okay, but I think you should at least tell you parents what you've decided to do when they visit this evening."

"I can do that, you know I feel better already."

I have no intention of telling my parents anything about the treatment. If I do they will find a way to stop it, even though I am of age to sign the consent. I have to try this, it might be my only chance at getting well. Maybe it also might get rid of the voice, I surely hope so. I can't sleep I'm so excited about beginning the shock. It's wonderful to think I could be like everyone else, once the treatment is over.

I had my first therapy today, and I am drifting in and out of reality. I just thought I was confused before, now I'm not sure of anything. Dr. Shannon assured me that tomorrow things would be a little clearer. I'm not sure I made the right decision at all. I will receive at least six treatments. The shock therapy is over, and I am home with medications for two weeks. I am scared of my shadow. Mother is sleeping with me every night. I'm having nightmares most every night. I can't remember how to do the smallest of things. Mother gives me strange looks, when she thinks I'm not aware. I think she might be a little afraid of me. I was wrong thinking I didn't have any memory before the shock.

This morning when I came down for breakfast, I heard Mother talking to someone on the phone. I quietly stood outside the kitchen door. I heard her ask Dr. Shannon, how long I would be in this state. I heard her say, oh, then it is the medication, are you saying she will get back to normal when the medicine is all gone. Thank you, Doctor it's such a relief to know things will get better I slipped silently back up to my room. I took the three bottles of pills, and flushed them down the toilet. I don't plan to tell anyone. Now hopefully, I can begin to unscramble my mind.

It's been two weeks since I threw my medication away, and I am beginning to feel human again. I'm sitting in Dr. Shannon's waiting room, debating with myself, wondering if I should tell him I threw away my medication.

"Hello Suzanna, it's good to see you, how are you feeling, you are looking good?"

"I just can't believe what you've done to me. I thought you really cared about me."

"What do you mean, Suzanna?"

"You didn't tell me the therapy would take away my whole life, I guess I might as well tell you the truth, I threw away all those pills you sent home with me. By the way, I'm thinking a lot more clearly without them. Don't even think about giving me any more."

"That's great, Suzanna, the sooner you get off the medication, the sooner you will get your short-term memory back."

"If that's the case, why did you give me the medicine in the first place?"

"Some people need the medication for a while. The ones that don't realize it and stop taking it just as you have done. You may not believe it, but you are on your way to being a stronger person. I'm very pleased with our results."

"Doctor how long will it be before I can remember the important things? There are so many blanks that I can't fill."

"Don't tax your memory trying to bring back the past, just take one day at a time. Remember the treatments purpose was to take away the things in your past that made you unhappy. I told you it would affect your short-term memory temporarily."

"How long before I can drive again?"

"You aren't on any medication now, so there is no reason you can't drive as of this moment. I know you feel lost at this point, but believe me; all the necessary things in life will come back automatically.

On our way home Mother asked if the Doctor was pleased with the results of my treatments.

"Yes, Mother, he says I'm just trying too hard to remember things. He says if I would just relax and give it time, things that are important to every day life will come back."

"That's so good to hear. I do want you to be okay dear it's been so long since you have felt well."

"Oh, I almost forgot Dr. Shannon says I can drive now too, since I'm not on medication."

"Oh, that is great, I know you would like to get out and about on your own again."

"Yes, it will be good to see Janet and "Little Bit. You know Mother until a few days ago, I'm sorry to say, I hadn't even thought about Janet. I wouldn't have her know that for anything in this world though."

"I know dear, but I think under the circumstances she would understand."

This morning I got up feeling great, it's been a long time since I've felt this good. When I walked into the kitchen, Mother looked up with a smile.

"Goodness, don't you look nice and chipper this morning. Are you hungry, how about some buttermilk pancakes for my favorite daughter?"

"Sure Mother," I said, "it's been years since you fixed me pancakes. What is the occasion?"

"Oh, you know it used to be your favorite breakfast when you were little."

We sat at the table, me eating my pancakes and Mother having her cup of coffee.

It felt so right, sitting there with Mother, I felt so warm and cozy I don't think I've ever had this closeness with Mother before.

"I'm going to visit Janet today, Mother."

"Okay honey, will you be back for supper?"

"Oh yeah, I'll be back before then."

Now here comes the real test I thought, driving out into the main road. Will I be able to find Janet's apartment complex? I drive through our beautiful little town, and I am surprised how things are coming back to me. Once I found the complex, I just automatically knew the exact location of Janet's place. I was a bit anxious ringing the bell though. What if it isn't the right apartment? I couldn't remember the number for the life of me. I gave a big sigh of relief when thank goodness the lady that opened the door was Janet.

"Suzanna," she cried, and hugged me so tightly, I thought my ribs would break. "I have been worried out of my mind, where have you been so long? Come on back to the kitchen, and I will put on a pot of coffee, we have so much to catch up on." We sat at the table, (yes, our very favorite place), and just looked at one another. Janet reached across the table and took my hands into her own. She squeezed them tightly and turned them over, my palms up, and then her eyes caught the scars on my wrists. Her mouth flew open in disbelief. "SUZANNA! WHAT HAVE YOU DONE TO YOURSELF?" I burst into tears and she began to cry with me. After a few moments I regained my composure, and told Janet all that I could remember about my stay in the hospital. "I'm going to need you to help me fill in the blanks in my life right now, Janet, do you think you can?"

"I don't know, but I'll give it my best, Suzanna."

"Doctor Shannon says I'm trying too hard, but he just doesn't know how lost I feel. I was afraid to drive over here, as many times as I've been here. I didn't even remember the number of you apartment, yet somehow I just knew this would be the right one."

"Whose bright idea was it for you to have shock treatment anyway, your parents I bet."

"No, it was all my idea; they didn't even know until I had, had my first treatment."

"I still can't understand why your mother didn't tell me you were in the hospital. Why I must have called a dozen times I know, and all she ever told me was you were not there."

"Janet, you know my folks were too embarrassed to tell anyone.

I was on the psychiatric floor of the hospital. If anyone had wanted to come to see me, they would find out my sickness was mental. That would be a shameful thing for someone like Daddy, you know.

"I guess you are right about that, but you have to promise me you will never try a stunt like that again. What on earth made you do such a thing, Suzanna? What happened to you that pushed you over the edge?"

"Honest to goodness, I don't know why I did it; I was hoping you might have an idea. Did I have something that big, bothering me that much, that I might have talked to you about?"

"I'm sorry, but I can't help you there, I had no idea you were that stressed about anything, at least you didn't talk to me about it."

"Janet please be honest, I surely must have told you something."

"Suzanna I am being honest, you didn't tell me anything, that was bad enough for you to try to take your on life. If I didn't see the scars with my own eyes, I wouldn't believe it. Have you talked to Bill since you got back home? Rick said every time they see each other, he ask about you. I guess if he called you, your mother told him the same thing she told me, nothing. Do you think Bill might be the reason you did what you did? Maybe y'all had a fight or something."

"You know I haven't even given a thought to Bill. We did go out that night. He had Sunday supper with us. I don't remember having a fight with him. If we did, I don't think he would be asking about me, do you? I don't think it would be fair to contact Bill now. I don't think he could possibly understand what's happened. I surely couldn't explain to him why I did such a terrible thing, since I don't know myself. I should have told him I was under the care of a physiatrist.

It wouldn't be fair to expect him to go on as if nothing has happened. It'll just be better for everyone concerned if we forget about our friendship."

"Suzanna, I thought you were in love with Bill."

"Did I tell you that, Janet?"

"Yes, you said if your folks didn't approve of Bill, you would marry him anyway, don't you remember Suzanna?"

"I must have been wrong then, because I wouldn't forget something as important as love, do you think?"

"I don't think anything could happen to me, so bad that I would forget I love Ricky?"

"So there," I said, "We can consider the subject closed?"

"Would it be alright if Rick tells Bill you've been in the hospital?"

"Yes, if Bill should ask about me again, just don't tell him why I was in the hospital."

"Oh no, you know we would never do that, Suzanna."

While Rick and Janet were eating the evening meal, Janet explained what had been going on with Suzanna. "I ask her if it would be alright for you to tell Bill she's been in the hospital, she said okay, just don't go into details. I told her we surely wouldn't do that. I think it only fair that Bill is told."

"What can I tell him, honey? I think Suzanna should be the one to talk to him."

"Rick, she can't, she doesn't even remember how much Bill meant to her."

"What am I supposed to say, Bill you remember Suzanna, well she went completely nuts. She just got out of the psycho ward. She doesn't ever want to see or talk to you again, however she doesn't know why she feels this way."

"Okay now, Rick, get real, don't you dare say Suzanna is nuts. Whatever you say, don't tell him she tried to kill herself. Just tell him she hasn't been well, and it might be a while before he hears from her."

"Okay honey, but I don't like to be put in this position. You know Bill's one of my best friends. It's just not right to keep him in the dark like this."

"I know honey, and I'm sorry I asked you to bring him here to meet Suzanna. I still think Suzanna and Bill are soul mates. Despite what she says, I believe they were more than friends. I know for a while Bill meant more than a friend to Suzanna, she just doesn't admit it."

"It was a lot more than friendship to Bill anyway," answered Rick.

"Really, tell me what he told you, plez-zzzz."

"I'm sorry honey, but I promised Bill I wouldn't tell anyone what he told me in confidence, and a promise is a promise the way I see it." Janet knew that tone of voice from Rick meant the subject is closed.

Chapter Sixteen

Rick and Bill ate lunch together the next day. Rick didn't know how to approach the subject of Suzanna, so he decided if Bill didn't bring her up, he sure wasn't. No sooner than the thought ran through his mind of course, Bill asked if they had heard from Suzanna.

"I'm not gonna beat around the bush, Bill, just last night, Janet told me Suzanna had come over. She said Suzanna has been in the hospital. I'm here to tell you, Janet was really ticked off with Suzanna's mother. And I kinda agree with Janet, the woman could have told Janet that Suzanna was in the hospital. I don't know what's going on, but from what Janet said, it wouldn't be a good idea for you to try to contact her right now. Something about she needs time to pull herself together from her illness."

"What do you think that means, Rick?"

"Beats me friend," answered Rick, shaking his head from side to side, women, what man can understand them anyway? Rick had no idea how upsetting this news was for Bill. Bill felt so guilty, what had he done to sweet Suzanna. Would he ever get a chance to make it up to her?

What was she in the hospital for, it would have been too early for an abortion, wouldn't it, he thought to himself.

"It's about time to get back to the grindstone, Bill, guess I'll see you tomorrow." Rick said, getting up from the table

"Huh, sure see you later Rick." Man thought Rick, Bill's got it bad for Suzanna, and it's all my fault, for introducing them in the first place. Janet and her fixing the world schemes, she thinks she's Cupid.

Chapter Seventeen

As summer turns into fall, I am feeling much better. But I think it is too soon to think about college. I just can't think about studying right now, what if I have forgotten all I ever learned in school? I'm still having a hard time believing, I agreed to shock treatment. Surely I wasn't that sick, or was I? My life is on hold right now, and I'm getting bored. I've decided to look for a job, maybe a part time one to begin with, just in case work isn't the answer. I'm not having any luck finding a part time job in this town. No one wants to hire me. It hasn't exactly been a boost to my confidence.

Just the other day I went to eat in the little restaurant on the square, well bless my heart, if there wasn't a help wanted sign in the window. I decided on the spur of the moment that I was going to apply for the job. I knew Mr. Burns, the owner, so I just walked in and told him I had come to apply for the job. At first he thought I was kidding, but then I told him I planned to go to college the first of next year. I explained to him I didn't want a permanent job, so if he would hire me just for a few months, I would be obliged to him. "I don't have any experience or anything," I said.

"Okay missy, just fill out the application, and report to work at eight in the morning," said Mr. Burns.

"Oh, thank you, Mr. Burns I promise you won't regret hiring me; I'll work really hard you'll see." I was so excited about getting the job that I completely forgot to eat lunch.

I could hardly wait to tell my folks, I had a job. The minute we sat down to eat supper, I blurted out, "Guess what, I got a job today."

"Honey that's just great, where will you be working, and what will you be doing?" Mother asked.

"You know the restaurant on the square, I will start to work there at eight o'clock in the morning."

"I didn't realize they had a hostess in that little place," was my mother's reply.

"Oh, they don't Mother, I'm going to be a waitress."

"Sure you are," laughed Daddy, "you know we won't allow you

to do such a menial job as that. It would be humiliating for my daughter to be a waitress. What would our neighbors think? Some of them would have a heyday spreading the word, I'm sure."

"I'm sorry you feel this way, Daddy, but I intend to go to work in the morning. You know I am of age now, and if you are going to be ashamed of me, I can always move out."

"Suzanna, Suzanna," her father said, shaking his head from side to side. "I'm not ashamed of you. I'm only trying to tell you that you are selling yourself short. You are much too smart to be a servant, you must know this. Please look for a real job. I know you can do better than this."

"I've given my application to every business in this town. They all want someone who will stay with them forever. When I tell them I plan to go to college next year, that ends the interview. So the only kind of job I can find temporally is this one."

"Well now," said my father, with a smile on his lips, "that puts a different light on things. You haven't told us that you are planning to go on to college. Under these circumstances, you are absolutely right, that kind of job will be fine for a few months, if you feel you must work."

"I am so pleased with you," said my mother. "Have you decided which college you might choose?"

"I'm still not absolutely sure, but I have plenty of time to decide."

Later in the evening, I lay on my bed thinking about our discussion at the supper table. I know that I shouldn't say this, but sometimes Daddy can be such a bigot. I don't know how Mother has managed to live with him all these years. Poor Mother lets him lead her around by the nose, most of the time. She is such a humble person really, and she can't stand to argue. I guess it's a shame that I didn't get any of her traits, but it's just not right for a man to feel superior to his wife, the way Daddy does. Had I been able to pick my parents, I would have never picked the ones I have.

Meanwhile, downstairs in the study, Mary and Frank are discussing the supper conversation.

"Frank, do you think Suzanna will keep her word and go to college next year?"

"We can always keep our fingers crossed, do you think she can hold a waitress job, Mary?"

"Sure, it should be natural for a woman to wait on tables," answered Mary. "Being a servant defiantly won't come natural to Suzanna, I can tell you that, Mary, you have been her servant since the day you got her. This subject is not worth discussing any longer,"

Frank snapped, opening his paper. Mary sighed, and picked up her book. Sometimes it seems he doesn't care about anyone but himself, she thought. Sometimes Frank doesn't seem like the person I married at all, maybe his business is worrying him. I don't think he would tell me if it is. He never talks about business with me. I guess he figures it would be over my head. I can be thankful for one thing though; he never scolds me for spending money. At least he has always provided for his family, never complaining, the way my sister Madge's husband does her. However he made the statement I was Suzanna's servant, I guess it hasn't dawned on him that I'm his servant too. He always knows how to make me feel guilty when it comes to Suzanna. He never puts it into words, but he knows I get the message just the same.

When I came down ready for work, bright and early the next morning, Mother's reaction was, "My don't you look spiffy, what would you like for breakfast?"

"I think I'll just have coffee and a piece of toast."

"Are you sure, dear, you know being a waitress can be tiring, you probably should eat more than toast."

"Goodness Mother, I've already got butterflies in my stomach. You make it sound like you know about being a waitress first hand."

"Maybe I do," she answered, "what do you think I am around here, if not a servant?"

"I'm sorry, I never thought of it that way, Mother. I guess you are absolutely right. I tell you what? From now on I will take care of my own needs. I wish I could speak for Daddy, but I don't think it would do any good."

"Not to worry honey, your daddy will always need a servant. I knew that the day I married him. I did marry him for better or worse though."

"Look at the time I gotta go, see you tonight, Mother."

"Bye honey, and good luck on your first day."

I put a big smile on my face and walked into the restaurant
"Here I am Mr. Burns, ready to go to work."

"Okay Suzanna, you have the smile so here is the apron to go with it," he chuckled. He took me back to the kitchen, and introduced me to the cook and the dishwasher. The cook is a man, his name is Nick, and his wife Joanne, is the dishwasher. They hardly looked up from their work, and kinda mumbled a hello. Then we walked back into the dinning room, just in time to see this tall, good-looking lady walk through the front door. She walked over to us, and Mr.

Burns said, "This is Lucy Jones, she's the one you will be working with, and she will teach you everything you need to know. Lucy, this is Suzanna Stoggins, she is here to fill the waitress job, for a few months, anyway, and then she will be going off to college. Suzanna doesn't have any experience, but with a teacher like you, I know she won't have any trouble learning."

"Thank you Mr. Burns, for your confidence," answered Lucy, and she tied on her apron.

"Now let's see girl, where should we begin?" mused Lucy, turning to face me.

"I hope I can catch on quickly, so I won't be a bother to you."

"Don't you worry your pretty little head, honey, there ain't nothing to this job. If I can do it anybody can, believe me."

I liked Lucy instantly, she is so friendly, and she's one of those people with what I call a bubbly personality. I sure hope she likes me. I don't see why Mr. Burns had to even mention the fact that I am going to college. I don't want her to get the wrong impression of me, that I'm some kind of know it all. I hope she will want to be my friend. She's so at ease and relaxed. I hope she will tell me her secret, and teach me to be the same.

Mother was right this job isn't going to be easy, especially on my feet. Lucy is being so patient with me. I never dreamed how much was involved in being just a servant. I feel like a dummy, I spilled a glass of water on my very first customer. It was so humiliating. I wiped up the spill apologizing repeatedly, and then I ran for the kitchen in tears. Lucy followed me, to try to make everything alright.

"Listen to me honey, you are going to have accidents in this kind of work, we all do. You did all you could to fix things. Anyways, Mrs. Simmons is a pleasant lady, and she's understanding about it being your first day and all. Now if it had been that grouchy old lady with her, it would be a horse of a different color. They come in here at least once a week, and I swear I ain't never seen that woman smile. For the life of me I don't know why they are friends, they's completely different from each other."

"But Lucy, will Mr. Burns understand, or will he fire me on my first day?"

"Heavens no child, he ain't gonna fire you for some little something like that."

"Tell me honestly Lucy, how am I really doing, will I ever be half as good a waitress as you?"

"Believe me, you are doing just fine; I never trained anyone before as quick to learn as you.

I know how tired you are right now, not being used to the job and all, so why don't you just sit down over here, and I'll go get you a coke or something."

Tears came into my eyes, as I thanked Lucy for being so compassionate. She came back with our cokes and sat across the little table from me. Then Lucy asked me why this job was so important to me. She said "I know a girl like you don't have to work, especially a low paying job such as this. I'm telling you, girl if I didn't have to work, I wouldn't be here, no sireee-bob."

"It seems as if you like it here Lucy, no one could tell otherwise by your actions."

"Don't get me wrong, Mr. Burns is a good man to work for, but if I had me an education like you, I wouldn't be here. Why without tips I couldn't make ends meet. I barely get by and I live in a dump, cause I can't do no better."

"I'm so sorry Lucy, I didn't know. You see, I wanted to see what it's like to work, and the businesses here in town only wanted permanent employees. So this was the only job I could find temporarily.

"Well child, you picked a dilly of a job to learn how it feels to work, that's all I can say. Here, you will shur-nuff learn what it's like to work for a living."

"You are right Lucy, I don't think it will be difficult to decide to go to college after working here."

"I know what you mean girl," and Lucy laughed with me.

When I got home from work my first day, I was dragging as I entered the kitchen, where Mother was preparing supper.

"Hey, how was your first day, dear?" I could tell the way she was looking at me that she knew I was dead on my feet.

"You were so right Mother, I didn't think today would ever end. I feel like an old woman, every bone in my body is tired."

"Now don't you be bad-mounting old women. Your mother is one you know," she said while patting me on the back.

"I'm sorry, Mother, but this day has been a wake-up experience for me. Please don't tell Daddy how worn out I am. I'm determined to hang in there somehow, until time to go to college. Lucy, the other waitress is an angel in disguise. I know you would like her. Bless her heart, she doesn't understand why I want to work there, any more than you do."

"Oh honey, just look at you, you are totally worn out, you know you don't have to keep this job."

"Yes I know, but I have to prove to Daddy that I'm not a quitter, and that I can persevere. I cupped my hand around my ear and said, "I think I hear a long hot shower calling me."

"I'll see you at supper, Mother."

At the table that evening, Daddy could hardly wait to grill me about my day.

"How was your first day at work, little girl, you did make a full day, or did you?" he laughed.

"I surely did make the whole day, and it was fun, and rewarding. Lucy, the other waitress, is so funny, and she says I'm a natural born servant. It gives me a good feeling, to serve other people." I looked across the table at Mother and winked. I wish I had applied for the job months ago."

For once in my life, Daddy was at a loss for words, and his expression was priceless. This is once he didn't get to say, I told you so. I excused myself early, eager to get in bed. I won't have any problem, sleeping tonight. I've never in my whole life been this tired. This bed has never felt better.

The next day at work wasn't quite as bad as the first, but it still wasn't that great. When Lucy and I sat down for our lunch, I was already so tired that I didn't feel that I could possibly make the rest of the day. I guess Lucy read my face, for she said, "penny for your thoughts."

"To be truthful Lucy, I was just wondering how you could possibly work this hard every day, with such a great attitude. My feet are killing me, and my head aches. I want to prove to myself and my daddy that I can do any job, no matter what, but you know right now, I'm not so sure I'm not a weakling after all."

"Now you listen to me child, it was just as hard for me at first, but your body can get used to anything, over time. Here," she extended her hand across the table, "take these aspirins for your head, and keep your chin up girl, I know you can do it. You got a headache from being so up tight all the time, that's all. Once you get more used to the job, you will relax, and your headaches will be gone on their own. You go get you some comfortable shoes, and your feet will quit hurting. Believe me when you have a week under your belt, you will know you can handle this job. I just don't see you as a quitter, girl." I sat silent for a moment, and thought over what Lucy had said. My eyes welled with tears, and I softly told her thank you for her pep talk. I knew without Lucy I wouldn't have the energy to work another day.

"That's what friends are for you know," said Lucy getting to her feet. It made me feel better, just to know that Lucy considered me her friend. Janet would like Lucy too, I thought going back to work.

When the day was finally through, I felt as whipped as the day before. I decided I would heed Lucy's advice, so I went and bought me some working shoes, before going home. They are not the prettiest things to look at, but they sure feel good to my poor tired feet. When I got home Mother was not there, just as well I thought, and I went upstairs to my room. I drew a tub of wonderfully hot water, poured in the bubble bath, and stepped in for a nice long soak.

I got so comfortable that I fell sound asleep. The next thing I knew Mother was calling my name. When I opened my eyes, and looked up, I saw the fear in my mother's face.

"Oh I'm so sorry I frightened you Mother, I was so beat when I got home, that I came right up to take a tub bath, to relax me; and it relaxed me alright, I fell sound asleep it seems. Please don't worry about me harming myself anymore, Mother, I promise you I will never do such a foolish thing again."

"Oh honey, Mother replied, with relief in her voice. When I couldn't get you to answer, then found you in the tub, it just brought back everything. How was your day, a lot better I hope? You look refreshed right now."

"Today was just as hard as yesterday, to tell you the truth; I would not have made it without Lucy's moral support."

"Please don't put yourself through this, quit the job and just relax until you go off to college," begged Mother," you don't have to do this."

"Yes I do Mother, for my own satisfaction; I have to keep this job. I'll be fine. I just have to get used to it. I bought myself some shoes today like Lucy wears. Promise you won't tell Daddy what a difficult time I'm having."

"Not to worry, my lips are sealed, but if he's the reason you think you have to stay with this job, give it some more thought, because your daddy wouldn't like any job you get, he wants you in college, period."

"Daddy knows I'm planning to go to college, he's just stubborn and wants everything his way. I looked at my mother's expression, and I knew what she was thinking. "I know, I guess I'm as stubborn as he is," I said with a smile.

"I'm going to fix supper now, Mother answered, why don't you take a nap, and get rested up for your daddy," and she returned my smile.

I got the surprise of my life; Daddy didn't even ask one question about my job, at the supper table tonight. Actually there was very little conversation at all. I suppose he could have had a problem with the business, or just a hard day. After desert, I helped Mother clear the table. When the kitchen was cleaned, Mother headed for the study, to be with Daddy. I told her I was going over to Janet's for a while. She asked me not to stay too late. I told her not to fret morning comes early, when one has a job.

When Mary entered the study, Frank was reading his paper like always. She sat in her favorite chair, and picked up her book. She knew Frank was watching her over his paper. Oh dear she thought, I hope he's not in a bad mood tonight. He put his paper down on the table beside his chair, and it seemed like minutes he just sat there staring at her. She could feel her face getting warm.

Finally he cleared his throat, and spoke gruffly, "Mary are you ready to tell me what's going on around here?"

"Why dear, what on earth are you talking about?"

"You know very well what I'm talking about, what's going on with you and Suzanna? I'll bet she has already quit that two-bit job, if the truth was known. How long were you two going to wait to tell me?"

"She has not quit her job. In fact she's really proud of herself. She's found a new friend, and that is a comfort to me. Suzanna is getting her life together, and I'm very proud of her, and you should be too. Our daughter is becoming a stronger person each day. She's proving to herself that she can make it in this world, all on her own if the need arises."

"Now Mary, you surely don't think she can support herself on the minimum wage. I think not, her pay check wouldn't buy her gas for her car, much less a place to live, and food to eat."

"Frank, you know that's not what I meant. Why don't you want her to be successful? Why can't you encourage her, rather than put her down? You are giving her the wrong impression of who you really are. Why can't you let her know the man that I know and love?"

"What are you saying Mary?"

"The man I know is gentle and loving, and provides for his family. He's a man that can be a real softie, almost childish at times. The man I know would give his life for his family. He's a man that expects too much of himself, and of others also. This man loves his daughter, as much as if she were his own flesh and blood. However he doesn't know how to show his daughter how much he loves her, therefore she feels she's a great disappointment to him."

Mary got up from her chair, and walked over to Frank. She gently pulled his head to her chest, and ran her fingers through his hair, and she softly said, "Dear I know it's not easy for you to show affection to Suzanna, but couldn't you stop being so critical?"

All he could manage to say, after clearing his throat was, "thank you for understanding Mary, I'm sorry and I'll try to do better in the future. You might have to remind me every now and then though, okay?"

"Sure I will honey. I'm tired, so I think I will go up to bed now," she whispered.

When I arrived at Janet's place, Rick was watching a Braves game. "How's the game," I asked.

"Man the braves are kicking butt tonight, Suzanna, how you been doing?" was his answer.

"Come on back to the kitchen, where we can talk in peace," said Janet. "What have you been doing lately? Just yesterday I was wondering if I had hurt your feelings about something, it's been so long since you've been over."

"Oh no, Janet, you know me better than that; I've got a job, I started working Monday. I never thought about how much of my time a job would take, until now. To tell you the truth, I've been going to bed by ten o'clock."

"Why I didn't know you were looking for a job, where are you working for goodness' sakes, what kind of job did you get?"

"In Daddy's opinion, it's just a menial job, going absolutely nowhere, but you know my daddy. I have a waitress job, up on the square."

Janet wrinkled her brow, trying to place the restaurant. "You know-o-o, the little restaurant Mr. Burns owns, the only eating place on the square actually."

"Oh yeah, I had almost forgotten we even had a restaurant here in town. Let's see now, what's the name of that little place?"

"John's Short Orders," is the name, I said.

"Heavens, Suzanna, I can't imagine you as a waitress. What in the world possessed you to get a job like that?"

"Watch it now Janet, you are beginning to sound just like Daddy. I thought you would understand, after all you know me better than anyone else."

"Wait a minute Suzanna, don't go getting defensive with me. I didn't mean any harm in what I said. You just caught me off guard that's all, and it's not easy to think of my best friend as a servant, you know."

"This is how important it is for me to be in charge of my own life. I didn't go out looking for a waitress job, mind you. All the other jobs here in town were permanent, and I've decided to go to college next year. I was just going in to get a bite to eat, when I saw a help wanted sign in the window. So I thought to myself, what the heck, why not, and I went in and applied for the job. Mr. Burns is a super nice fellow, and he said I could have the job, if I really wanted it. He didn't think I was serious to begin with, and I don't think he expects me to be there for long, but he's in for a surprise."

"Gosh, isn't it awfully hard work, Suzanna?"

"I would be lying if I said it isn't, but Lucy, the other waitress is helpful and encouraging. I'd say she's in her thirties, and she has very little education, but she is such a good person. I would have walked out, probably the first day, if it hadn't been for her, and most certainly the second day."

"Maybe I'll just drop by one day and meet this Lucy," said Janet.

"I wish you would. She just seems so much wiser than her years, and she always knows how to make a person feel better. She's one of those people who's in love with life."

"I'm glad to hear you have decided to go on to college, friend. Sometimes I wish I had, had the chance to go, but it's a little late for me now."

"Well it's not Janet, there are lots of people who go to college after they are married."

"I know, but it would be useless for me to go. Rick don't want me to work, he is one of those men that think men should earn the living, and women should stay home an raise the family to be honest with you Suzanna, I don't want to work; I like staying home with "Little Bit.""

"To each his own, whatever makes you happy is my thought on that. I'd better head for home, as it's almost ten o'clock. When you slave every day, you have to get your rest." I laughed.

"Guess what," Janet said sitting on the couch beside Rick

"What?" asked Rick, although he wasn't the least bit interested, after all couldn't Janet see he was trying to watch TV.

90

"Suzanna has a job. You'll never guess what it is, never in a million years."

"Since you know I can't guess, why don't you just tell me," he answered, trying to see who hit the home run. It never fails, he thought when I'm trying to concentrate on something, is when Janet needs to communicate with me. "She is working at "John's Short Orders" restaurant, get this, as a waitress mind you. Can you believe that? I'm telling you, Rick, I will never understand how that girl's mind works. Why in this world would anyone who has everything they could ever want take a job waiting on people?"

"Maybe it's easier to work when you know you don't have to, honey." Rick answered.

"Now you know you may be right, but she did tell me one good thing, she is going to college next year. I just hope she doesn't change her mind again." Janet got up from the couch, stretched and yawned. I'm tired, I think I will go to bed and read a while. She didn't see the big grin on Rick's face, before she left the room. Now, he thinks I can watch the game in peace.

In my second week of work, I was clearing off a table, when I realized I was not as tired as usual, after working half a day. Lucy was right about the shoes; my feet were not hurting at all.

And come to think of it, my head wasn't hurting either. Lucy came over to say it was time for our Lunch break.

Lucy looked across the table at me with one of her cheerful smiles. "Why are you giving me that smile?" I asked.

"I was just thinking, how you don't look or act like a new girl anymore. I told you it ain't that hard, you just got to get the knack of it, that's all," Lucy answered.

"You were absolutely right, Lucy, You told me my body would adjust, and my headaches would go away, and they have.

I can't believe it's lunch time already, and I don't feel tired at all."

"You're in just your second week too. You've done a lot better than I did when I first came to work here. But then I was a good bit older than you are though."

"If I'm not being to nosey, how old are you, Lucy?"

"Let's just say, I know life don't begin at forty," she laughed.

91

"Nooo-way, you can't be over forty, why you don't even look thirty-five."

"Oh honey, you have made my day. Why if I had it to spare, I'd give you a twenty. You are a sweetheart Suzanna, that's what you are."

I was clearing our table, when the bell on the door got my attention. I couldn't help but notice how good-looking the guy was as he sat down at a table. Lucy motioned for me to take his order.

I noticed he wasn't wearing a wedding band I wondered if he lived here in town, I was too shy to ask him. When I went back to the kitchen to place his order, I didn't realize my face was flushed. Lucy asked, "Did he say something out of the way to you." I told her it wasn't anything like that. I asked her if she knew his name, and had she seen him here before. Her answer was," honey if you want to know his name, just ask him."

"Oh Lucy I couldn't do that, but if you take his food out to him, you could ask for me."

"No, no I can't do that, 'cause if you decided later you don't like him, then you would blame me for the whole thing."

"No I wouldn't, please Lucy, do this one favor, and I'll never ask you for anything else."

"I'm sorry, but if it's gonna happen, that you get with him, it will have to happen on its own, I don't get mixed-up in nobody's private life, uh-uh, never."

So when the order was ready, I took it to his table. I gave him my sweetest smile, when I placed his plate in front of him. "Would you like anything else, I all but whispered?"

"Yes he said, returning my smile, I would like some catsup please."

When I returned with the catsup and placed it on his table, his eyes met mine.

"Are you new in town, I think I would remember if I had seen you before," he said.

"No, I've lived here most of my life. Do you live here?" I answered.

"Yes, I live here, my name is Lester Little; I work over at the Chevrolet Dealership. I'm a mechanic that's why I'm kinda dirty right now," he apologized.

"My name is Suzanna Stoggins, and this is my second week working here, it's nice to meet you Lester."

"Same here," was his answer. I could feel his eyes follow me, when I walked away from his table I saw Lucy's great big smile coming to meet me. Her first words were, "see there girl; you didn't need no help from me, I knew you could do it. Now what is his name? When are you two going out?"

"His name is Lester Little, but he didn't ask me out. He apologized for the grease on his clothes. He says he's a mechanic, over at the Chevrolet place, across the street."

"I can tell there is interest on both sides here, so I know he will ask you for a date, and I wonder what your answer will be," mused Lucy.

"I don't know, but the next move is up to him. I just want to know, how you know he's interested in me, just by looking at him, Lucy?"

"Oh I know that look honey, oh yeah; I've had my times too, you know," she laughed.

Lester motioned to me, pointing to his tea glass. While I poured his tea, he asked, "Would you like to see a picture show with me sometimes?"

"Sure why not," I answered.

"How about tonight then, or is that too short notice?" he asked.

"I don't have any plans for tonight, so I suppose we could go tonight," I said, and I gave him directions to my house.

When I cleared his table, he had left a five-dollar tip; no one else has ever been that generous. I wondered what kind of guy he would turn out to be. Then an old fear popped into my mind, that maybe I'm making another mistake, like with Fred. I know he's at least four or five years older than me. I'm a lot smarter about men now, and surely I can handle it, if he does turn out to be another Fred.

I hurried home after work, to get ready for my date with Lester. When I came into the kitchen, I told Mother, I wouldn't be eating supper tonight. If I hurry I will have time to soak in a bath, and wash my hair too. I quickly stepped into the bath, and settled in, and then I heard Mother knock on my bedroom door.

93

"Come on in, I'm in the tub," I said. Mother entered the bedroom, noticing the bathroom door ajar; she peered around the bathroom door, to speak.

"What happened today dear, why are you in such a hurry?"

"Oh, I met this guy in the restaurant he asked me out tonight. He is just soooo handsome His name is Lester Little, I assume he lives here. He's a mechanic at the Chevrolet Dealership, the one just across the street from the restaurant

"I don't recall ever hearing the name Little about town," mused Mother.

"Now Mother, please don't start, just keep in mind I am eighteen now, and you said yourself, just the other day that you were pleased with the way I am growing up, finally."

"I don't mean to be nosey, but dear I am concerned, because I love you. Try to understand how I feel, Suzanna."

"Oh, alright, Mother, just don't start worrying about me. I really can take care of myself. I promise I won't do anything you wouldn't do, okay."

"I'll go on back down and start supper now, are you sure you don't want to eat before you leave?"

"Yes Mother, I'm sure, I simply won't have time to eat, I still have to get dressed and do my hair."

I can say one thing for Lester, he is prompt, he rung the bell right on the hour. I knew he was handsome in the restaurant grease and all, but after a good clean up, he is simply gorgeous.

His hair is so black it's blue in the sunlight. His eyes are as blue as the sky, just before a rain. He kinda reminds me of Elvis, I wonder if anyone has ever told him before that he looks like Elvis. His aftershave is just breath taking, in a nice kind of way. He just sparkles with cleanliness. Even after taking so much time with my own appearance, I feel down right drab, compared to Lester.

Chapter Eighteen

When we were driving down our drive, the very first question Lester asked was, "You are of age I hope."

"I'm eighteen," I answered, thinking uh-oh, here we go again with the age thing.

"I reckon you've finished high school and all," was his next reply.

"Yes, this past year was my last; I'm going to college next year."

"I didn't go to college. I got this job at the Chevrolet place right out of high school. I was lucky really. They even sent me to school to learn my trade. They said I just had the knack to be a mechanic. What are you going to do when you finish college?"

"I have no earthly idea what I want to do, or if I will even finish," I said.

"Girls don't need to go to college, unless they want to be a doctor or something like that. Course that's just my own way of thinking."

At that remark, I decided it was time to change the subject. I got his opinion loud and clear on women, so I asked him how long he had been working at his job.

"Let's see, I'm twenty five now, I was twenty when I finished high school, so that makes it five years about now."

"My," I said, "lots of people are married by the time they are your age, or have been married."

"I just ain't met the right person yet, I guess you could say," he answered. "Why do you ask, you wouldn't be out husband hunting, would you?"

"Heavens no, I'm not sure I ever want to get married," I laughed.

I was pleasantly surprised that Lester was a complete gentleman, and I enjoyed being with him. I will admit though, he's not one I would want to introduce to my folks, not hardly.

When Lester walked me to my door tonight, he took my hand in his, looked into my eyes, and thanked me for a good evening. No goodnight kiss, no asking for another date, just saying, "I'll call you later."

This left me a little miffed, although I knew Lester wasn't Mr. Right, as Janet would say.

However I wondered if he really would call me again.

The next morning at work, Lucy wanted to know all about my date.

"It really wasn't that exciting. He left me with the impression that, like Daddy, he thinks women are second-rate citizens.

"What do you mean, Suzanna, what does your daddy think about women?"

"Oh you know. Women are not as important as men. They are here mostly to serve men, like cooking, cleaning, and entertaining guest, that kind of stuff."

"So you think that's how your daddy thinks about you and your mother, huh?"

"Yeah, Lucy, I think that sums it up rather well."

"Little miss, you tell me why your daddy wants you to go to college, thinking that's how he really feels about you."

"Actually, I think he wants me to go to college, to find the right kind of husband. He thinks men who don't have a college degree will never amount to anything. Daddy figures if I stay around this little town, I'll end up marring someone like Lester."

"Even though you don't agree with all of Lester's views, you are gonna give him another chance ain't you?" asked Lucy.

"What do you think, Lucy, should I give him another date, that is if he calls?"

"All I know is he is awfully good looking, course sometimes that don't count for nothing.

Specially if they thinks they are God's gift to women, and they knows how good they look."

"I probably shouldn't put him in the same category with Daddy, at least until I know him a little better.

I'm not sure he wants to go out with me again. When he told me goodnight, he just said he would call me later."

"There is something bad wrong with him, if he don't want to go out with you no more, is all I'm gonna say," answered Lucy.

When I got home from work, Mother was out this was a relief, because I didn't want to talk about last night. All I wanted was a good hot shower, and a long nap.

Supper was over and I was helping clear away the dishes, I sensed that Mother wanted to ask about last night, I couldn't imagine what she was waiting on. The situation was making me edgy so I finally blurted out, "Mother what would you like to know about last night, I know you are full of questions, so let's just get it over with."

"You are right dear, I would like for you to tell me about last night, but only if you really want to."

I could hardly believe my ears I had never had a choice before. Mother was trying to let me find my independence, something I didn't think was possible for her to do. So I replied: "It was uneventful, in fact almost boring, to tell the truth. We really don't have anything in common."

"I'm sorry, it seemed he made quite an impression on you. You seemed so excited, when you were getting ready last evening, what changed your mind?"

"I guess it was because he was so handsome, but I find that's all he has going for him, is his good looks. I started thinking about it, and I know some of the prettiest girls were the shallowest, back in high school."

"So I guess you won't be seeing him anymore," Mother said.

"I'm not sure, he said he would call me, and Lucy says I should give him the benefit of the doubt."

"I hope you won't let Lucy influence you, unless you are a hundred percent in agreement with what she says."

"Mother, you know me better than that, I'm too stubborn to let anyone influence me, without my agreement anyway."

Mary entered the study where Frank is reading his paper as usual. "Honey, could we talk," she asked?

"Sure, what's on your mind?"

"I was just talking with Suzanna, about the new boy she met. Do you know any Littles in town?"

"I can't say that I do, Mary, do you know anything other than his name that I might relate to?"

"He works at the Chevrolet place, across from the restaurant, but Suzanna is not sure if he lives here in town."

"Is he in sales?"

"No, she says he is a mechanic. I have the feeling he is a good bit older than Suzanna."

"All I can say is I'll be glad when it's time for her to go to college," said Frank.

"I just hope she doesn't change her mind again about going," sighed Mary.

"What did she say to make you think she might change her mind, about school?"

"She hasn't said anything exact, but she hasn't mentioned going lately either. We will need to do some shopping before time for her to leave."

"Do you think this new guy will change her mind?"

"No, thank goodness, she said the only attributes he has, is his good looks. She doesn't seem to think he will even call her again."

"That's a relief," answered Frank, picking up his paper. This gesture was a dismissal for

Mary, so she got up from her chair, and quietly left the room. I guess I'll have to ask Suzanna about college, she thought. If only we could have seen the future, when we took Suzanna as our own. Thanks to us, she will probably need counseling for the rest of her life. If I had only known, I could have prevented so much of her pain and confusion. Tears ran down Mary's face as she climbed the stairs to her bedroom. She would always feel the gilt, even if she lived to be a hundred.

I have become almost as good as Lucy, on the job. Lucy and I are the best of friends. We go to the picture show, almost every week. Lucy can always make me feel better, no matter what my problem is. We are both aware I have only six more weeks to work, before going off to school.

We never talk about, it though. It's like we both think if we don't talk about it, it will go away.

"Well look who just come in the door, girl," said Lucy.

I looked up from the table I was clearing, to see Lester coming toward me with that marvelous smile. Yes, I thought, he even has perfect teeth.

"Hey, Suzanna, I've been planning to call you, but something always comes up. I thought I'd just drop by in person. How about a date tonight, I know it's short notice and all, that is if you don't have something else planned."

I told him Lucy and I were going to the show tonight, (this is a little white lie), but I told him I would be free tomorrow night.

"Okay tomorrow night it is," he said, "See you then around six," then he turned and sauntered out the door. When Lucy was sure Lester was out of hearing distance, she said, "Why did you lie to that man like that, I was almost tempted to tell him I would go with him. I couldn't though, after you told him I was gonna be with you."

"Come on Lucy, I didn't want him to think he could ignore me for weeks, then expect me to jump at an hour's notice, to go out with him again."

"Oh my goodness, I didn't think of it that way; you were absolutely right," said Lucy.

"Lucy let me say this, if you want to make a play for Lester, you go right ahead, it won't bother me in the least."

"Don't be silly, you know I was just kidding," laughed Lucy. "Why I could be his momma."

"What time you want to meet me at the picture show," I asked.

"Oh, we really are going," she asked.

"Yeah, we are going, you know I'm not a liar. I told Lester we were going, so unless there is some good reason you can't go, I'll meet you there."

"We already been once this week, I'm not sure I can afford to go again, Suzanna."

"Come on, the treats on me. I'm the one that got us into this mess in the first place."

"Alright then," said Lucy," I'll see you around eight, out in the lobby."

Driving home my meandering mind turned to Lucy. I never would have dreamed anyone's budget was so tight that they couldn't go to the picture show more than once a week. Without a doubt that has convinced me that I definitely will go to college. I should have thought about Lucy's way of life, before now. I could have been paying her way all those times. I know how small my paycheck is, but I just assumed Lucy made more than I did, because, after all, she's been there for years. I could never live on my wages, and I really don't know how Lucy does it. I know one thing though; from now on the treat is on me.

Chapter Nineteen

Lester was prompt as usual, picking me up for our date. I couldn't help but almost stare as we drove he's so pleasing to the eye. I wish he had the personality to go along with his good looks.

"I've been thinking," he said, "you and your friend have already seen the picture show that's playing, so there is no reason for you to have to see it again tonight."

"That's up to you Lester, if you want to see the picture, then I won't mind watching it again."

"I don't care about it, in fact I would rather do something else. It being Friday, we don't have to get up early for work tomorrow, why don't we go dancing?"

"Where around here can we go dancing, Lester?"

"Goodness, don't you know about Spring Hill Inn, you said you've lived here all your life, I'm surprised you never been to Spring Hill Inn."

"I don't think I've ever even heard of it, how far out of town is it?"

"Oh, I'd say it's about five miles north, going toward Atlanta."

"Then you have been there before, Lester?"

"Shoot yeah, I've been there lots of times, it'll be loads of fun, Suzanna."

When we drove into the parking lot, I couldn't believe my eyes. The building was way off the main highway down into the woods. It didn't look like it had ever seen a can of paint. I couldn't imagine what it looked like inside, nor could I believe Lester would even think about bringing a date here. He jumped out of the car and came around to open my door.

"Come on girl, let's go shake a leg."

"You've brought other dates here before, Lester?"

"Sure lots of times, what's with you anyway, Suzanna?"

"Do they allow drinking in there?"

"Yeah, big deal, I'm of age, and so are you."

"I want you to take me home, Lester."

"What's got into you, Suzanna, I came to dance, so get your butt out of the car, and come on."

I was frightened, the place looked like a dump all of a sudden I didn't feel all grown up anymore.

"I want to go home please," and I began to cry, while he continued to yank on my hand.

He loosened his grip, and dropped my hand then he went to his side of the car, and got in. Before I could shut my door, he spun out of the drive. We drove for a minute in silence, then he said: "I want to know why you have been leading me on. You are old enough to know, teasing can be dangerous. If you ain't I'm telling you now."

"But I haven't been teasing and leading you on," I stammered.

"Oh, not much you ain't. Don't tell me you don't know what your eyes are telling me, when you look at me the way you do."

"What are my eyes telling you, Lester?"

"Your eyes tell me you want me, all of me. So why can't we see where things will lead, and if it don't work out, neither of us will be any the worse for it. Nothing ventured, nothing gained, is the old saying."

"You have certainly read my eyes wrong, Lester, if I've led you to believe I care for you that way, all I can say is, I'm very sorry. Now will you please take me home."

"Okay, so we are from two different worlds. You just count yourself lucky that I am a gentleman. I am going to take you home now, without making any demands of you."

"I can't agree that you are a gentleman. A decent person never would have put me in this situation," I snapped.

"Just shut-up, Suzanna! Don't push your luck; I don't want to hear anymore of your whining. I just want you out of my life, I hope I never lay eyes on you again."

"That you can count on, Lester," I screamed.

* * *

Later as I lay safely in my bed, I had a long cry. I thought I had all the answers, that I am a mature, and intelligent person. I thought I was strong enough to go out on my own, that I could handle any situation. Then tonight I was as frightened as a little girl. At least what happened tonight has helped me decide which college I will choose. I will go to the all girl college where Janet went to high school. I will feel safe there, and it's not that far from home. I won't have to go shopping for clothes, because they wear uniforms, in that little north Georgia school.

I made my announcement about the college I had chosen, at the breakfast table the next morning.

"That's wonderful dear," said Mother, we must start shopping for your wardrobe right away."

"That won't be necessary, Mother, they wear uniforms, so I won't be needing any new things."

"It was my understanding, you said you were going to a junior college, and live here at home," was her daddy's comment.

"I did say that, but I believe it will be cheaper than our local college, in fact I know it will."

"Why do you think that?" asked her father.

"All the extra clothes, and make-up I won't be needing, for one thing."

"If that's really what you want, it's fine with me, but you know money is not an issue," said Frank.

"Yes, I realize that, thanks for understanding, Daddy."

"We will miss you so much if you go away," said Mary.

"Now, Mother, it's not that far away. If I wanted to, I could even come home on weekends. I need to gain my independence you said that yourself, you have been my servant long enough."

* * *

I walked into the restaurant my head held high, and a smile on my face. I would never tell anyone what happened Friday night not even my best friend Janet.

"Hey, girl, you look like the cat that swallowed the canary," quipped Lucy.

"Gosh Lucy, where do you come up with all these quaint sayings?"

"I don't know, I've just heard most of them all my life. You musta had a great weekend, with a smile like that."

"Oh no, believe me, my weekend isn't worth talking about, how was yours?"

"Ditto child, I didn't even get out of the house."

"What, you mean you didn't go to church, Lucy?"

"Yeah, I did go to church, I just didn't feel good at all over the whole weekend."

I'm sorry, do you feel okay now?"

"Yeah, I guess it was just one of them viruses, or something, I'm fine today."

I couldn't help but notice; Lucy just wasn't herself. She didn't have good balance at times. She swayed when she walked, and she would have to hold on to the table she was cleaning. When we walked out at quitting time, I asked Lucy if she still didn't feel well. The answer I received was: "Why you ask that honey, I'm fine."

"I thought we were friends Lucy, but I guess I was wrong."

"Now what in the world does that mean, you know we are friends."

"Friends don't lie to each other, that's what I mean, Lucy."

Lucy looked at me, tears welling in her pretty brown eyes. She spoke hardly above a whisper. "The truth is I'm real sick, but there ain't nothing nobody can do to help me."

"Why can't something be done, what is wrong Lucy?"

"I've got leukemia."

"Oh no, how long have you known about it?"

"I guess about two weeks now, nigh on to that anyways."

"What did your doctor suggest you do?"

"He said I could take something called chemo, I told him no, I don't want too."

"Why not, Lucy, do you want to die?"

"The doctor says, it just makes you sicker, and all my hair will fall out most likely."

"Lucy, you have to try, you can't just give up. You once told me I wasn't a quitter, I don't see you as a quitter either."

"Honey, the chemo is not gonna cure me, it might give me a few more years, but I probably would be too sick to even work, and you know I have to work."

"Look at it this way, Lucy, while it's giving you a little more time, it will also give science more time to find a cure, don't you see?"

"Suzanna, you know I can't afford all them fancy treatments, even if I wanted to."

"Is that the only reason you told the doctor you didn't want the treatment?"

"Yeah, that's one reason, and the other is I just don't want to get too sick to work."

"Daddy has connections to a lot of charities, I just know he can get you the help you need."

"You can't ask your daddy to help somebody he don't even know."

"Lucy, just tell me, if you had the money would you consider taking the treatment?"

"I might think about it, I ain't real sure though."

"If you decide you will try it, then I will find a way for you to get help."

"You would really do that for me, wouldn't you, you are a sweet girl Suzanna."

"I need your answer tomorrow, so Daddy can get right on it."

"I ain't never had a friend like you before," Lucy said, and she embraced me.

"You've been just as good a friend to me, and I know you would do the same for me," I answered.

At the supper table, I approached Daddy. "I need your help with a problem," I told him.

"Okay, Suzanna, let's hear your problem."

"My friend Lucy needs financial help, I don't know how to get it for her, but I told her you would know."

"You are old enough to know better than to get involved with other people's money problems. When people know you are financially well off, they will take advantage of you, even those you call friends."

"You don't even know what I'm talking about, but right away you start judging my friend. I'm sorry, I will never understand your way of thinking, Daddy." With those words I got up from the table, and headed for the stairs. Just as I stepped on the bottom step, I heard Mother call to me.

"Wait honey, give your daddy a chance to understand, explain it to him. Frank, you sit and listen to what Suzanna has to say, before you make anymore comments."

I turned and looked at Mother; why I had never heard her take such a firm stand against Daddy!

I walked back to my place at the table, and sat down, "thank you Mother."

Then I turned to look at Daddy. He looked at me, and a small smile crossed his lips, and he said: "Yes your mother does know how to assert herself, when the need arises. I see how shocked you are, but this time your mother is absolutely right. So now you have my full attention, tell me the whole story. I'm sorry I jumped to conclusions. I admit that is a bad habit of mine, please forgive me."

I took a deep breath, wondering if I was dreaming, and I began: "My friend has leukemia. She can't afford chemo. I told her I would help her find the help she needs. I knew you would know how to do this. If it comes down to it, I will work and pay for her treatment."

"This friend means that much to you?"

"She does, if not for her, I would have never made it on my job."

"I'm so proud of you, Suzanna, that you know the value of friendship. I do know how to get your friend the help she needs. I will get on it first thing in the morning. You tell her not to worry about expenses any more." I jumped up from my chair and ran to hug Daddy.

"Thank you so much, you will never know how much this means to me. I'll never forget your kindness. I'll always love you for this deed," I said, a tear running down my chin Then Mother chirped, "who wants cherry pie a la-mode for desert?" Leave it to my dear mother to fill in when things get awkward.

I couldn't sleep for hours after I went to bed. I was so excited about the good news I had for Lucy. I got to work early to have time to talk with Lucy, before our day started. Then it dawned on me, possibly Lucy wouldn't want the treatment. Then what, I don't know anyone who has had chemo. I can't be sure it's the right thing to do. I'm not qualified to advise her, one way or the other.

106

When I arrived Lucy wasn't there, Mr. Burns told me, she had called in sick. It was the first time Lucy had been out sick since I came to work here. The day was terribly long and hard for me. I couldn't keep my mind on what I was doing, for worrying about Lucy.

It finally got around to time to leave work, and I rushed to my car. I've decided to go by Lucy's house and check on her, maybe she needs something. I knocked on the front door, over and over, but there was no answer. I turned the knob and it opened. I stepped inside and called out to Lucy but there was only silence. I had visited Lucy many times, so I walked down the little hall, to her bedroom. The door was ajar, and I could see Lucy lying on the bed. I thought she was asleep, so I quietly walked over to the bed. I didn't want to frighten her, so instead of calling her name I touched her arm. "Lucy," I whispered, she didn't move or open her eyes. I felt for her pulse then I ran from the room. I found the phone on the sofa, and dialed the operator, "Please help me," I cried when the operator answered. I can't remember how I managed to drive home after the ambulance came and took Lucy's body. I couldn't stop crying, I had never lost anyone to death before, and I felt almost unbearable pain. When I got home Mother put me to bed and promised she would call Dr. Shannon. I couldn't sleep, and I didn't want to eat. Mother called the doctor, and he said he would be by after his last patient.

I guess it was some where around eight o'clock when Mother brought Dr. Shannon to my room.

"Suzanna," he called and lightly knocked on my door. "May I come in, he asked as he turned the knob?" He stepped into the room, and I could feel his eyes on me, lying on the bed. I didn't move or say a word. He walked over and sat on the side of my bed.

He reached and lightly touched my hand. I turned to face him, and started to cry all over again.

He took my hand in his, and he began to rub my arm ever so gently, then he spoke, "Go ahead, cry as long as you need to child."

I sat up beside him and continued to sob, he put his arm around my shoulder I pressed my face against his chest. All my tears were finally spent, and I found my voice.

"Doctor I feel so empty, every time I get someone in my life, I really like, something always happens to them. I must be evil or something. It's true I do still have my best friend, but it's not like it used to be, before she got married. Fred came along in my life I didn't see things his way, so he left and never came back. Then there was Bill. I can't remember why he doesn't come around any more. Then I found a job and met Lucy. She was such a good person, and a great friend. She didn't even tell me she was sick, until the day before I found her dead. I can't help but believe I have a curse on me. What have I done so terrible that this is happening?"

"No, no, there is no such thing as a curse. You know Suzanna; there is a reason for all things that happen in our lives. We don't always understand it, but we will eventually. You have to stop blaming yourself, for every bad thing that happens to the people in your life. I thought you were going away to school, did you change your mind?"

"No, I decided to work for a while, and start school the first of next year. I don't guess I have a job now, because I haven't bothered to call Mr. Burns. I really don't think I could ever go back to the restaurant again."

"Do you feel you need a little rest in the hospital, Suzanna, if so I will arrange it."

"No I really don't think that is necessary, however I could use some medication. Just for a few days until I can pull myself together."

"Sure I'll write you a prescription, you take it as long as you need, and if you need to talk to me, you just call anytime. You must eat to feel better you do realize this don't you? Your physical health has all to do with your mental health, don't ever forget that."

"I know doctor, but I've just lost my appetite completely. I will never understand why someone as good, and as young as Lucy had to die."

"There is a lot in our lives we never understand Suzanna, but we still have to go on and do the best we can. When you get through with this medication, I want you to call and make an appointment. We need to talk some more when you are feeling better."

* * *

It's been two weeks, and here I sit across the desk from Dr. Shannon. He asks if I feel better now, or will I need a few more weeks of medication. "I think I'm going to be okay now. I called Mr. Burns, and he seemed to understand when I told him I wouldn't be back I've never lost anyone before. Lucy was special she could make me laugh at myself. She never tried to change my mind about anything, the way everyone else does. Lucy was different from anyone I've ever known--always happy and laughing. She lifted my spirits when I was at my lowest. I was counting on having Lucy as a friend for years to come, and then wham, just like that, she is gone forever."

"Suzanna, this is a part of life, you will be losing people you love, for the rest of your life. The first time it happens is the hardest. I'm not saying you will ever get used to giving up loved-ones, nor will it ever be easy."

"Sure Doctor. I understand I won't ever get used to it. I can promise you one thing though; I won't ever attempt to take my own life again. I know now how hard it is for the ones left behind."

"Look there, something good has come out of your loss already. It's given you a different outlook on the value of life. You've quit thinking about yourself first, and put others before you. Yes Suzanna, I can see now what a valuable friend Lucy was."

I left that session with Dr. Shannon, with much to think about. I had never seen myself as self-centered or self-pitying before. Me. Pampered me, I can have anything I ask for, and I still feel sorry for myself. Janet has been so right about things. She hurt my feelings, or sometimes made me angry, but it was because she was right on target. I'm so ashamed, it took the death of such a dear friend, for me to see the truth about myself. I'm going to turn this page in my life and start all over. There will be no more procrastination it is time to live my life to the fullest. I'm going home and start packing for college. There won't be any more excuses for not getting a good education. I feel like a heavy weight has been lifted from my shoulders.

When I reached home, and started into the house, I looked up at the beautiful night sky and whispered, "thank you Lucy, for being a part of my life, I will never forget you."

Chapter Twenty

When I entered the house, I peeked around the study door, and just like every other evening, that's where I found my parents. Mother looked up from her book.

"I just stopped to say I'm home, sorry to disturb you Mother."

"How are you feeling dear, you did see Dr. Shannon today, didn't you?"

"Yes, and we had a great session today, I'm going up to start packing for school now."

"I could come up and help with your packing, if you want me to," answered Mother.

"Sure if you want, come on up, but if you are reading a good book, don't feel you have to help me."

Mother's eyes lit up, and she replied, "Great I'll only be a minute, let me get to a stopping place in my book."

Frank took his paper down from his face, and looked at Mary, with a frown in his brow, "Are you sure that was our daughter, that just left this room Mary?"

"I was wondering the very same thing, Frank."

"Get on up there before she has second thoughts, and changes her mind," said Frank.

Mother stood in my door, like she wasn't sure if she should come in. She had a puzzled look on her face. "Come on in, Mother, sit here on the bed and we will talk," I said as I patted the bed beside me.

"Okay," she answered, now let's see, what shall we talk about? When do you plan to leave for the college?"

"Let's see, I'll need to see Janet one day. Today is Thursday, I should be ready to drive up on Sunday, if nothing happens."

"Are you sure you don't need more time to think about things, before you go, dear?"

"Things are going to be different from now on, Mother. I'm not going to be self-centered any more. I'm not going to go around feeling sorry for myself, blaming everybody else for my problems. It's terrible that it took the death of a close and dear friend to make me take a good long look at myself. When I get back for a visit, I hope you will meet a completely different Suzanna. I know it won't be easy to change, but I'm going to give it my best."

Mother's mouth flew open in astonishment, "You are a perfectly lovely person, why there is no reason whatsoever for you to try to change."

"No Mother, you of all people wouldn't see anything wrong with me, I promise you though, you are going to like the new me much better."

I finished my packing, and got ready for bed. I drifted off to sleep with a feeling of peace within.

The next morning, right after breakfast, I headed over to Janet's house. We sat out beside the Kiddies' pool, so "Little Bit" could play while we talked.

"So Suzanna, just like that," she snapped her fingers, "you are off to school."

"Yes, I answered, don't you think it's about time I made one decision on my own?"

"Yeah, I do, but are you sure about being alone, especially right now?" asked Janet.

"I'm sure Janet, more sure than I've ever been of anything in my life. I've been soul-searching, and believe me; I don't like what I found. I wanted to ask you, why you didn't point out my faults to me, you know me better than I know myself probably."

"Why Suzanna, I don't know what you are talking about."

"We've been friends most of our lives, and you sit here and lie to me like this, Janet?"

"That's it, we are best friends, and I don't think you have that many faults, I never have," Janet answered.

"Janet I lost a very dear friend in Lucy; I don't want to lose you too."

"I don't think I could bear ever losing you, for any reason either," said Janet.

"You have to help me become a better person, by being truthful, Janet. You know I like to feel sorry for myself. You must love me like a sister, to stay best friends with me. I want you to know, I'm thankful for your friendship, but you simply have to start being honest with me. It's for my own benefit, can't you see that, Janet?"

"Yeah, I think I know what you are saying, but being a best friend, in my opinion, is accepting each other for what we are, and never trying to change anything. You have qualities I like, that made me want you for a friend."

"We were just children, when we became friends, Janet."

"I know, but you still have lots of traits I like about you. I fail to see that much wrong with the person you are right now. We all could be better, I guess, but I don't want you to become a stranger, Suzanna."

"Oh, I could never become a stranger to you, I just want you to promise to point out my faults, so that I can correct them. Is that asking too much of a friend?"

"No, if that's what you really want, I'll try. But I'm gonna tell you right up front, I like myself just the way I am, so don't ever try to return the favor," laughed Janet.

"Very well Janet, I'll try not to help you become a better person," and I laughed with her.

"So are you going to call Bill, and tell him you are leaving?"

"No, I don't see any reason to call Bill; if he wanted to hear from me, he has my phone number."

"Rick says, Bill's still asking about you, and if you want to know what I think, you two belong together."

"Come on Janet, don't start on that soul mate thing again."

"Okay, just maybe you will meet someone, away at school, I can hope, can't I," Janet asked.

"Just don't hold your breath, okay," I answered.

"How often are you planning to come home for visits? It's not that far you know?"

"I don't think I will be coming home soon, I need time away from everyone."

"Even me, your best friend, we will see you at Christmas, I hope?"

"I don't know when I will be back home, but I'll call you the minute I get here."

"Please do, and if you ever get bored, maybe you could write to me," Janet asked, pursing her lips.

"Maybe," I smiled and embraced her. "I really must go now, and get the car packed."

When I walked away from the pool, I could feel Janet's eyes on me, I turned and waved, a tear rolled down my cheek. I wonder if my life will ever be as happy as Janet's, maybe just maybe.

* * *

Sunday evening after supper, Janet sat down beside Rick on the couch. He was watching sports on TV as usual.

"I guess Suzanna has arrived at Berry by now, it's after two o'clock. She couldn't have picked a lovelier place to go. It's so peaceful there maybe she will find what she's looking for, before she comes back home.

"Do you think she knows what she's looking for?" asked Rick.

"That's what worries me the most honey, I don't think she does," Janet said, with tears welling up.

"Now Janet, don't start, you have done everything humanly possible to help her."

"I know, but I am her best friend, and I feel like I've let her down, somewhere along the way."

"You are not a doctor, and you are not responsible for her happiness, or her well-being."

"I know that Rick, but reminding me don't make me feel any better. Honey does Bill still ask about her?"

"Matter of fact, he hasn't talked to me about anything in a long time."

"I guess it's a little awkward for him to think of something besides her, to talk about with you."

"Yeah, I guess it would be, since I'm the one that introduced him to heartache. You know honey, I think she hurt Bill really badly."

"Why do you think that, is that what he told you, Rick?"

"Not in so many words, but something has changed him a lot."

"Do you think he might like to know she went off to school?"

"I don't see what good it would do him, Janet."

"We-l-l, it might make him think that is why she hasn't called him."

"Janet, I know where this is leading, so just stop right where you are. We are not gonna get involved with anymore of Suzanna's romances, no--ma'am."

"Please honey, I know they are good for each other. It might just take a nudge from us, to get them back together. All you would have to do is ask Bill if he's heard from her. When he says no, you could say, I guess you know she went off to college. This would give you a chance to see how he feels about her now, please honey, do it for me," pleaded Janet.

"No way, I won't help set Bill up for another fall. The subject is closed, Janet, there is a movie coming on I want to see."

Janet got up and left the room. She wasn't going to give up that easily, not when it concerned her best friend.

Chapter Twenty-One

I was excited about leaving on Sunday morning, so I was up early. I've had a hard time trying to explain to my folks that I'm not sure when I will be back for a visit. They don't seem to understand that I need to get away for a while, to heal emotionally. I can't help but believe that distance from this place, where all my sorrow happened, will help me heal faster. But I couldn't bring myself to tell my parents this. Even if I had voiced this, they wouldn't understand.

At times I don't feel any close ties to my folks. I wonder if other people have these feelings from time to time. This is an area I can't compare with Janet, since her mother died so young, and she never even knew her daddy.

I arrived sooner than I expected. There was no one in the registration office, I sure am glad I called ahead, to know which dorm I'm assigned to. While I unpacked, my thoughts went back to the time Janet went to high school here. I looked around the room it was huge for one person, and I have a feeling I'm gonna be lonely by myself. Sure hope I can find a roommate, soon.

I think I'll go for a walk before dark. I can finish unpacking later. Hopefully I will meet someone to talk to. I walked along the stone path; it was still just as beautiful as when I visited Janet here. Couples were sitting on the grass under the shade of the beautiful big magnolia trees laughing and talking. As I watched them, it brought back the weekend in the park, with Bill. I felt the tears coming, and I dropped my eyes to the ground, hoping no one would notice.

I brushed away my tears with my hand. Then all of a sudden I was almost knocked off balance. I felt strong hands grab my arms to prevent me from falling.

"Oh goodness," I cried, "I wasn't looking where I was going." I could feel my face flush with embarrassment. I looked up into his eyes.

"Hey, that's alright," he answered, "anyone as beautiful as you can run me over any time. My name is Tony, what may I call you fair maiden?"

"My name is Suzanna, I'm so terribly sorry, I should have been more alert."

"I haven't seen you around before, I know if I had I would certainly remember seeing a beautiful face like yours," he said.

"No, I just arrived today. I wanted to take a walk around the campus, before dark. I visited my best friend here, about two years ago, I think it's the most beautiful campus I've ever seen."

"It is and peaceful too," he answered, "so you are a freshman huh? I'm a junior, over at the boys school, I want to be a doctor."

"That's great, are you gonna be a specialist or just a regular M.D.?"

"To tell the truth, I haven't thought that far ahead, do you know what you want to major in?"

"No, I'm just going to wait until I make my first two years, then maybe it will come to me out of the blue." I laughed. My main reason for being here is because Daddy wants me to continue my education. You know how that goes, gotta try to make Daddy happy.

He looked at his watch then at me, "it's about time for the bus back to our dorm. I sure would like to see you again. Do you know the procedures on dating here?" he inquired.

"Heavens no, I didn't know there were procedures for dating, any place."

"There is here, I will write to you, asking for a date. So that means I need your last name to be sure you get the letter. That is if you will consider a date with me."

"My last name is Stoggins, and yes, I would like to see you again too."

He pulled a pen and paper from his shirt pocket, and wrote my name down.

"I've got to go now; you will be hearing from me soon," he said, and hurried away to the front entrance.

Tony had barley left my side, before this very attractive girl walked up to me. She had the most beautiful strawberry blond hair, and the greenest eyes. She must have contacts, I thought.

She was maybe five feet tall, and she might weigh eighty pounds soaking wet. I felt like a giant standing beside her, and I had always been the smallest one in my high school.

"You don't waste any time, now do you?" she asked.

"Excuse me, what do you mean, do I know you?" Oh dear, I thought this probably is Tony's girl-friend, what do I do now?

"I saw you run into Tony, to get his attention," she replied.

"If you saw it, then you know it was an accident," I curtly answered.

"So be it," she laughed, "my name is Ruth Grimes, who are you, may I ask?"

"I'm Suzanna Stoggins, I just arrived today, is Tony your boy friend?"

"I wish, no Tony don't belong to anyone at the moment. What hall are you on Suzanna?"

"I'm in Clair Hall, on the second floor, where are you Ruth?"

"It's a small world, I'm in Clair Hall too only I'm on the third floor. I've only been here a short time myself. Maybe we could be friends. Where did you get a name like Suzanna, it's gotta be southern right?"

"Yeah, I'm from a little biddy town just south of Atlanta, I'm not sure it's even on the map."

"That's okay," answered Ruth, "I'm from a little north Georgia town, and I'm almost sure it's not on the map. I'll bet we got a lot in common don't you?"

"Tell me Ruth, why did you make that comment about Tony?"

"Oh Suzanna, all us girls have tried to get Tony's attention. 'Course none of us were as smart as you, we didn't think about trying to knock him off his feet."

"I didn't bump into him on purpose, you've got to believe me. If you saw it happen, you know I'm telling the truth, now admit it."

"Maybe, I'm not sure yet about that, Suzanna. I'll have to get to know you a little better to agree with you."

"Why do you think all the girls here feel the way you do about Tony?" I asked.

"Didn't you look at him, Suzanna? He's the best-looking guy on this mountain that's all. He turns all the girls heads, even the ones with boy friends. Now don't tell me you didn't even notice how handsome he is. Why he could be in the movies he's so good-looking.

"I've seen other guys just as handsome. He didn't seem to be aware of his looks, the way most guys are."

"What did y'all talk about, Suzanna?"

"He told me he would like to see me again, and I would be hearing from him. He said something about dating procedures that I didn't understand."

"Oh yeah, if you want a date here, you have to write a letter to the person and ask. Everything has to be prim and proper, you know."

"It all just sounds so strange to me," I said.

"You do know the boys college is five miles from here, don't you?"

"I hadn't given any thought about guys being here at all. In fact the reason I chose this college is because it is an all girl college."

"Uh-O, sounds like you are running from a broken heart."

"Not exactly, I'm just not ready for a relationship right now."

"So," said Ruth, "Tony was writing your name on that paper, that means he will be sending you a letter, asking for a date next Sunday, more than likely."

"How in this world, Ruth, would you know when he might want to see me?"

"That's easy, Sunday afternoon is the only time, you can have a caller, on this campus."

"I see, how about off the campus?" I asked.

"I guess you could meet someone in town, but you would have to be back in, and the lights out by ten o'clock. You also have to get an approved pass to catch the bus into town."

"My, they really do believe in keeping us safe here, don't they?"

"Yeah," answered Ruth, making a funny face, "they mean no harm with all their rules, so they say."

"I'm not complaining. It's just that I've always had the freedom to go and come as I pleased at home. It will take some getting used to, but I can adjust."

"Tell me, Suzanna, will you go out with Tony if he asks you?"

"I'm not sure yet, I probably will, at least once."

"I hear the dinner bell," said Ruth, "come on, let's go eat, I'm starving."

We took a seat at one of the long beautiful tables, at that moment the voice whispered that this is where I belong, everything is so orderly. We said grace, and then everyone started passing the food. I hope maybe the voice will just evaporate here into the quietness, and reverence in this place. It's not with me as much as before the shock treatments, but it still sneaks in now and then.

We walked back to Claire Hall after the meal was over. When we got to the second floor landing in front of my room, I invited Ruth to come in and visit for a while. Ruth looked around and said, "I see you don't have a room-mate either do you?"

"No I don't, I wish I knew someone here to room with me though. These are huge rooms to be alone in, I imagine they can be awfully dark at night too."

"You're right about that, it's like a big old castle, there's all kinds of noise all through the night. I'm not a scary-cat Suzanna, but I surely hate the nights here."

"I've got the feeling that I'm gonna be the same way Ruth. Do you think we could ask the house-mother if we could room together, that is if you would want to be my room-mate?"

"Oh that would be great Suzanna, let's go ask Miss Reece, right now. Miss Reece gave us permission and said we could pick either room we preferred. We decided on my second floor room, and started moving Ruth in right away. We had to rush to finish before lights out time. Thank goodness I wouldn't have to spend one night here alone.

The next few days were hectic. I had to get my schedule worked out, and learn where all my classes were located. There were little cottages scattered all over the huge campus, and these were where our classes were held. There definitely wasn't any time to waste between classes. I almost needed a map to find some of the cottages because they were not close together. Some were such a distance apart that you almost had to run to make it on time for the next class.

I had been so busy getting used to the place I hadn't given Tony a thought. Then on Friday evening, when I got to my room, after my last class, there was a letter at the door.

I picked it up and slipped it out of the envelope, still not thinking about it being from Tony.

I unfolded it and read:

Dear Suzanna,

I would like to see you this Sunday afternoon. The bus will arrive at the entrance around two o'clock. I hope you will meet me there. I am looking forward to seeing you again. If by chance for some reason you can't see me, call the boys school, and tell the dean. There won't be time to send me your answer by letter. I'm sorry I waited until the last minute to send this letter, but this has been a full week for me

Your friend,
Tony

P.S. I hope to see you on Sunday.

Just as I was putting the letter back in the envelope, I heard Ruth rushing up the stairs. You could identify Ruth before you saw her; she was in a hurry all the time. Now I know why she's so tiny. She looked at the letter in my hand and gave me her cute little grin.

"Hey, look what we got, it's gotta be from Tony, right," she asked.

"Right, but where is the we coming from," I asked.

She puckered up her lips, and said, "come on now can't I come along? After all I saw him first."

"You know I wouldn't mind if you came along, but I don't know what Tony would think."

"Hey, you know I'm just clowning around, why I wouldn't dare go along with you."

"But it's true, you did see him first," I replied.

"Sure, but the difference is, he didn't notice me," she said, "however after you see him, if you decide he's just not what you are looking for, just mention my name to him, okay?"

"Sure, I'll just say, Tony I'm not a bit interested in you, but my room-mate is crazy about you. By the way her name is Ruth, and she'll be waiting to hear from you."

"You could word it a little differently, but that would be better than nothing," laughed Ruth.

"Oh, just get out of here Ruth, you are a clown."

We went to church on Sunday morning, but I couldn't tell anyone what the sermon was about, I'm ashamed to admit, but Tony was all that my mind could contain. While walking back to the dorm, Ruth chatted on and on. I guess she finally realized she was talking to herself, as far as I was concerned. All of a sudden I heard her scream, 'SUZANNA, you haven't heard a thing I've said, have you?"

"Ruth I'm so sorry, I guess my mind was wandering. What were you saying?"

"You guess, why I bet you haven't heard a word I've said the whole time we've been walking. What's wrong with you anyway, and don't say nothing. I've never seen you so distracted before. I'll bet you didn't hear a word of the sermon either, did you"

"To be honest, I didn't, and I feel bad about it," I said.

"Come on, you can tell me what's wrong, after all I am your friend and room-mate."

"There's nothing wrong, I've just been trying to decide why Tony is interested in me. I'm just an ordinary person, and I know I don't have a charismatic personality. Maybe he thinks I ran into him purposely. If that is it, he must think I'm the most forward girl he's ever met. He might even think I'm easy, what do you think, Ruth?"

"Oh, so Tony is on your mind after all. All I can say is, if you think he got the wrong impression of you, you can just explain it to him, the way you did to me, when you meet him this afternoon." I know it wasn't my figure that caught his eye, not in these frumpy uniforms.

They are a pretty shade of blue, but that's all you can say for them. The shoes are even worse, they are granny style, honest they have about an inch heel, and they lace up, and if that isn't bad enough, they are white, with brown heels. Even a beauty queen wouldn't be noticed in these outfits. Makeup is a definite no, no so appearance couldn't have been the reason Tony had noticed me.

Chapter Twenty-Two

I'm a nervous wreck standing here in the entrance, waiting for the bus. The other girls waiting here are laughing and joking with each other. It's like Janet has said a thousand times, I guess I am just too serious about life. You would think my life depended on making a good impression on Tony. Why once I know him, I might not even like him, so what is the big deal anyway. I have got to get control and relax, like everyone else.

When the bus drove up, I found myself moving back into the shadows of the big beautiful arches. When Tony came down the steps, I noticed for the first time, how handsome he was. His hair is sandy blond his eyes a sky blue. His complexion is the color of deliciously browned rolls. He is at least six foot tall. I could feel my palms sweating, when he reached for my hand.

We walked along one of the stone paths.

"I didn't think the afternoon would ever get here," he said.

I smiled at him, and reclaimed my hand. I was at a loss for words. I felt I was about to cry. I knew if I tried to speak, my voice would tremble. I had never felt so foolish before. I could feel my eyes began to moisten, and a lump was in my throat. Then I realized, we had stopped walking, and we were standing facing one another. He had a bewildered look, and seemed lost for words. I knew I had to get control of my emotions it wasn't fair to make Tony uncomfortable like this.

"Why don't we go sit under the magnolia tree over there, it looks so cool, don't you think, Tony?"

"Sure," he said. We sat down and turned to face each other.

"I'm sorry if I seemed forward, taking your hand in mine at the bus stop. I didn't mean anything by it believe me, Suzanna."

"Oh, that's not what's wrong," I answered. "You see; I started thinking that maybe you thought I bumped into you on purpose last week. I wondered what kind of person you would think I am. Take my word for it, I'm not nearly that bold, Tony."

"If that's what is bothering you, you can relax this minute, I know without a doubt, you didn't bump into me on purpose."

"How can you be so certain?" I asked.

"When I saw how distracted you were, I purposely ran into you. I had been watching you, and racking my brain for a way to meet you. When you turned down the path toward me, then I knew this was my chance. I don't have a line, like a lot of guys, to get a girl's attention. That approach is just too superficial for me."

"Alright," I gave a big sigh of relief. "I feel so much better, now that's out in the open."

"I know what you mean," he said. "Now we can take a deep breath, and start over getting acquainted."

We talked with ease it was like we had know one another for years. I could feel the trust we had between us. He was one of the most interesting people I had ever met. I knew he would make an excellent doctor one day. When we said goodbye at the bus, he kissed me gently on my forehead, and promised to come back the next Sunday.

* * *

The minute I entered my room, Ruth started her interrogation. "Gracious, Ruth, let me get my breath, will you?"

"It's been the longest afternoon in my life, I can't wait to hear all about your date. So start at the beginning, and tell me everything. Did he kiss you?"

"Ruth, you are not going to believe this, he said he bumped into me on purpose."

"No kidding!"

"Yes, he said he didn't know any other way to meet me, you know he's like me, he's kinda shy."

"Come on, Suzanna, a man that handsome can't be shy. Didn't he make your heart beat faster, just being with him?"

"Not really, I hear the dinner bell, come on let's go eat."

"Cute Suzanna, just change the subject won't you," said Ruth, and she giggled.

Right after dinner, before touching my homework, I decided to write a letter to Janet. I felt guilty that I hadn't already let her hear from me. Until now I didn't have anything interesting to write. I didn't want to write too much about Ruth, I was afraid Janet would think I was replacing her, this I would never do of course. Now that Tony is in the picture, I can make Ruth less important, in my letters. There were five pages before I finished, I'll be looking forward to her reply.

Rick didn't get in the door good, from work, before Janet started telling him about the letter she received from Suzanna.

"Honey, I got a five page letter from Suzanna today, can you believe that?"

"Then I guess she's doing okay, to have that much to write about?"

"Yeah, she is in great spirits, and thank goodness she's already found a room-mate."

"Why was it important for her to find a room-mate?"

"Because Rick, you know how depressed she gets at times. I didn't want her to have to be alone. Believe me, those big old rooms can be awful gloomy, even when you are happy."

"Oh, I keep forgetting that's where you went to high school ain't it," snapped Rick.

"You know very well I did, why are you being so sarcastic anyway?"

"I'm sorry, honey, it just seems you care more about Suzanna, and what she's doing, than you do about me, and "Little Bit.""

"Why that is ridiculous, and you know it; you are not being fair, Rick."

"Have it your way, like always, I'm gonna get a shower now," he answered and walked away.

Later while they were eating the evening meal, Janet tried to approach Rick again about the letter.

"There's one thing about Suzanna's letter that bothers me a little."

"Oh yeah, and what is that," Rick asked, halfheartedly.

"She's met this boy, Tony, and he seems to have made a big impression on her. In fact I've never heard her speak so highly about anyone she's ever dated before."

"So, what's wrong with that, I thought you wanted her to find

124

someone and get married, and have a life like yours?"

"I do want her to be happily married, but I still think Bill is the one to make her happy. I want her to give Bill another chance. By the way, do you two ever talk anymore?"

"Yeah, we still talk, but not about Suzanna."

"Has he found someone else?"

"I have no idea, and I'm not gonna ask him either. Janet, you need to stay out of Suzanna's life."

"Excuse me, we have been friends almost all our lives. She needs me and I need her. She's the sister I never had, and I love her. I'm not in her life, I'm a part of her life, and she's a part of mine, whether you like it or not."

"I beg your pardon, I forgot I am not allowed to have an opinion, when it comes to Suzanna."

"Now Ricky, you are being a butt tonight. This is not like you at all, are you not feeling well?"

"Nope, I'm just tired of hearing Suzanna every day. Before you got her letter, you wondered why she didn't write. I heard that every day, now you got a letter, and that's still all I hear, Suzanna, Suzanna, Suzanna."

"Why I do believe you are jealous of my best friend!" exclaimed Janet.

"No I'm not, but should I be Janet?" he shouted, leaving the table and heading for the TV.

Janet was furious. She stacked the dishes, and threw them in the sink, breaking most of them. I'll show him, she thought. The very idea of a husband being jealous, of his wife's best friend. After all Suzanna has done for us too. She wiped the table off, and got her pen and paper to answer Suzanna's letter. She sat there fuming, and then she realized she couldn't write a letter in her present frame of mind. She marched into the living room, and picked "Little Bit" up from her playpen and proceeded to go to the bathroom, to give the baby her bath.

She played with the baby in the tub, and this put her in a much better mood. After the baby's bath she sat in the rocking chair, and sang her to sleep. By the time she put the baby down for the night, her anger was spent.

She stood looking at her beautiful little one, and thanking God for such a perfect gift.

Rick walked up behind her, wrapped his arms around her, and drew her close. Janet felt her knees get weak, and her heart raced. This is what made her life complete. She would answer Suzanna's letter tomorrow, while Rick was at work. Rick was probably right. She did talk about Suzanna, an awful lot. Rick just didn't realize how much she worried about her friend. Suzanna needed her to help make her strong and independent. Come what may, Janet planned to always be there for her. I received Janet's letter, and I'll have to admit it did make me a little homesick. I had promised myself that I would try to stay away from home for a year maybe. I realized that I should have already called Mother, or at least wrote to her. I decided to go down to the office and call her as soon as I finished the letter to Janet. Janet's letter was interesting, but of course she wanted to know every little detail about Tony. I knew she would be disappointed when I told her that I didn't feel anything but friendship, where Tony was concerned. True we did see each other every Sunday afternoon, and we never tired of talking about any and everything. I don't have any romantic feelings for Tony at this time. If he feels more than friendship, he hasn't voiced it yet. Of course he has a lot more schooling, before he could even think about a commitment. I will be happy just to always be his friend.

I finished my letter, and headed for the office to use the phone. I dialed my number and the phone rang several times, before someone picked up. That's unusual for Mother to wait so long, to answer. I was beginning to think I dialed the wrong number. Just as I started to hang up, someone picked up the receiver.

"Hello, is that you Mother?"

"Suzanna, it's so good to hear your voice. Why did you wait so long to call, dear?"

"I've just been so busy, time flies here, I meant to write you a letter, but knew it might be a while before I could find the time, so calling seemed like the best thing to do."

"Oh, I would rather hear your voice than to get a letter anyway. How is school going, dear?"

"I just love it here. I don't know why I put it off so long."

"I'm so glad to hear you are happy there, honey, when do you think you will be coming home to visit. We miss you terribly, you know."

"It's not too long until Thanksgiving, maybe I can come then."

"That will be great, but it's still over two weeks away, try to call me again before then, okay?"

"Why Mother, is there something wrong?"

"No, I just need to hear your voice; the house is so quite without you."

"It's good to hear your voice too, Mother, I do miss you and Daddy. I'm gonna have to say goodbye now; I still have another class before supper."

"Okay, but promise me you will call again real soon, and I will be looking for you on Thanksgiving."

"I promise, Mother, I love you, see you at Thanksgiving, goodbye."

I hung up the phone with hesitation, my eyes misting with tears. Why do I always feel as though something is missing, in my connection with Mother? I know Mother loves me, but we have never had the closeness that I need so badly. I wonder if Mother feels something is missing in our relationship the way I do, or is it just my imagination. Maybe I'm just making a mountain out of a molehill.

While I am on my way to my next class, my mind wanders to Miss Mays, my English teacher.

I help her keep her silver polished, and she has loads of it. I do some of her heavy cleaning, and I also do her ironing. This school has a policy that every student has to have at least two days a week work detail. Miss Mays has taught me so much. She is from England, and a firm believer in having the best of manners. Not ever being married, she agrees with my theory that all women don't need marriage and children, to have a full and happy life. She's been trying to sway me, toward the teaching profession. I've promised her I would give it serious thought.

Chapter Twenty-Three

Tony and I are sitting under our favorite magnolia tree. We've been munching on cheese and crackers, and drinking white grape juice. It's been several minutes since either of us has spoken. We are almost as comfortable in silence, as an old married couple. I look across at Tony, wondering what he might be thinking about. It's making me feel uneasy for the first time, since we have know each other. He looked up, "Is something wrong, Suzanna?"

"Excuse me," I said.

"My goodness, where were you when I spoke, you had the strangest expression on your face, what were you thinking, if I might ask?"

"I was wondering what you are doing the long weekend of Thanksgiving?" I have no idea why I said this, for it definitely wasn't what I was thinking.

"I guess I'll just hang around here, and get in some extra studying, what are your plans?"

"I'm going home to visit my parents, I've never been away at Thanksgiving, and they think I have to be there. Don't your folks celebrate Thanksgiving?"

"They do most of the time, but this year Mom and Dad are going on a cruise. My older sister invited me to come visit her, but I don't really want to."

"Why, if I'm not being too nosey?" I asked.

"I just don't like my sister's husband that much."

"Why, Tony, I can't imagine you disliking anyone, he must really be an air head."

"He is kinda, we just don't have anything in common, other than my sister."

"My folks wouldn't care if you wanted to come home with me," I said.

"Thanks for asking, but I really do need some extra time for my studies. A long weekend of studying is just what the doctor ordered," he laughed.

When time came to walk with Tony, back to the bus, I found myself feeling a little depressed.

I wouldn't be seeing him for a good while, since this coming weekend was Thanksgiving. When we reached the bus, I quickly rose up on tiptoes, and kissed him on the cheek. Tony was caught completely off guard; he looked at me and asked, "Are you sure nothing is wrong?"

"Oh no," I said as I looked at the ground, "It will be a while before we see each other again, I will miss you, that's all."

"I will miss you too," he answered, and he lifted my chin in his hand, and bent over and kissed me on my lips, ever so softly.

"Goodbye Tony," I whispered.

"I'll write you a letter before you leave for the holiday," he called from the bus window.

When I entered my room, Ruth was gazing out the window, in deep thought, it seemed. I quietly crossed the room, and lay down across my bed. Ruth turned and looked at me.

"Suzanna, what is wrong? You and Tony didn't have a fight, I hope."

"No, Ruth, what would make you think that, for goodness' sake?"

"You know, you usually come in talking about the nice time you had, and all the things you two talked about. Then today, you just walk in and don't say a word."

"This afternoon was just different, I can't explain it, but my feelings for Tony today seemed different somehow."

"Oh, I see, what you are saying is you are falling in love with him. Suzanna, that is just wonderful."

"I'm not sure it's love Ruth, it's more a feeling of dread, as if I might never see him again."

"Why in this world would you feel like that, was Tony distant toward you or something?"

"No, he was the same as always, but I'm gonna have to give my feelings some serious thought, and see if I will find the answer. I hate this heavy heart feeling."

The bell rang for supper, and we headed for the dinning hall. Ruth tried to reassure me that things were going to be alright.

"Maybe you are coming down with a virus, or maybe you need

129

more rest." Ruth said. I didn't make any comment, but I knew she was wrong. I just couldn't explain the dread I felt, a feeling I had never experienced before. The next evening I received the letter from Tony. My hands were shaking so badly, I could hardly open the envelope. My feelings were beginning to frighten me.

What if I'm having a relapse? I decided I would see Dr. Shannon when I get home. I finally got the letter out of the envelope.

Dearest Suzanna,

I don't know what happened to you Sunday evening, but it concerns me greatly. Several times when we've been together, I've felt that I was falling in love with you. I've never got the same message from you--that is until Sunday. If I misread you on this, please tell me before you leave for the holiday. I want you as a friend in my life always, even if you can never be more to me.

We both know, it will be at least four more years, before we could get married. So if you don't love me now, you will have plenty of time to change your mind. (HA!) Kidding aside, Suzanna, I need to know where our friendship stands with you.

Forever yours,
Tony

I sat at my desk, trying to answer Tony's letter. This was the hardest thing I had ever had to do. How could I tell him how I felt, if I wasn't sure myself? I wished I could wait until I could see him again, to try to explain. But he asked for an answer before I went home.

Dear Tony,

I'm sorry, but I don't know how to begin this letter. Yes, I agree, something did change with us on Sunday. I'm just not sure what it means. There was a moment, when we were waiting for the bus, that I had the strongest feeling that I would never see you again. Our friendship means the world to me too. I don't know if I'm in love with you. I do know that

I will always want you in my life as a friend. We have a lot to talk about, on our next Sunday together. There are some personal things I need to tell you about myself.

Your Forever Friend,
Suzanna

I didn't go to the dinning hall that evening; I needed some time alone to have a long needed cry. I wished there was a way for me to stay here for the holiday, but I knew I would never be able to convince my parents, to accept my absence. I had a strong feeling that I needed to be here for Tony. Then the day before I left for home, I received a note from Tony.

Dearest Suzanna,
Thank you so much for your letter. You made my day. I'm sure there is nothing personal about your life that would ever change my love for you. I realize one would have to give a lot of thought to being a doctor's wife, but you have all the time you need, to decide.

I love you,
Tony

Tony had declared his love for me, but what if I can't return that love? I examined my inner most feelings for him, on my drive home. My mind swirled in circles, but it never calmed to a decision either way. I was completely confused and exhausted by the time I reached home.

With all the rig-mo-roe with Tony all week, I had forgotten to tell my best friend, Janet, that I would be home for Thanksgiving.

Chapter Twenty-Four

After Mother hugged and carried-on for fifteen minutes, I excused myself to go up and take a shower. I took as long as possible, hoping to relax a little, before going down to be bombarded by questions. When I came down, I found Mother in the kitchen as usual.

"There's my girl, I was beginning to think, you were sneaking a nap in on me. You do look a little tired, maybe you should take a short nap before supper."

"No, Mother, I'm fine, the shower revived me. Can I help you with something?"

"No, no, you just sit over there, and tell me all about school."

"There's not much to tell, except I have lots of work to do. It sure is a lot more difficult than high school, I can tell you that."

"You are getting good grades, aren't you, Suzanna?"

"Uh-huh, you haven't changed a bit have you Mother?" I laughed.

"Have you decided what career you will choose yet?"

"I know this will surprise you, Mother, I am thinking about being a teacher."

"Oh, Suzanna, I'm so glad, you will make a wonderful teacher."

"Not trying to change the subject, Mother, but do you think it would be possible for me to see Dr. Shannon, while I'm home?"

"I don't know if he went out of town, for the holidays or not, but if he didn't I'm sure he would see you. You are not getting sick again are you, dear?"

"No, I don't think so, Mother, I'm just a little mixed-up right now. I think I'll call his home and see if he's there."

I went into the study and looked up the doctor's number. The phone began to ring, as I held my breath, hoping upon hope that the doctor would be home. "Hello," I was in luck; it was Dr. Shannon himself answering the phone.

"Hello, doctor, this is Suzanna."

"How are you doing, Suzanna, home for the holiday I see."

"Yes, but I need to talk to you Dr. Shannon."

"My office is closed until next Monday, how long will you be home, Suzanna?"

"I have to go back Sunday, in time for classes on Monday. I realize this is an inconvenience doctor, but I really do need to talk to you. Could you meet me at your office later tonight?"

"Sure, Suzanna, I understand; I'll meet you at the office around nine o'clock, okay?"

"Okay, I'll be there thanks so much, you are a life saver."

When I returned to the kitchen, I told Mother I was going to see Dr. Shannon at nine.

"Very good, now let's put our heads together, and decide what we will fix for Thanksgiving dinner," said Mother. We had the menu all planned, and supper ready by the time Daddy got home. I ran and hugged Daddy, his face flushed as always, when I touched him. In return, he patted me on the shoulder, and managed to say I was looking good. Mother told him to go wash up for supper, giving him a chance to escape.

When we were seated at the table, I couldn't help but notice that nothing had changed since I had been away. Mother still seemed to change to someone else, when Daddy was around. I helped Mother clear the table after the meal was over, and then I excused myself to go freshen up for my appointment, with Dr. Shannon. I took a long and leisurely bath. I couldn't believe how much energy the last few days had taken. I was almost as tired after the bath as before. I have to take advantage of this time, with Dr. Shannon. He just has to shed some light on this for me. I surely hope it will be like my other visits, if so I will feel a lot better, once I've talked with him. While driving to his office, I tried my best to decide how to begin the conversation. I felt like I might have an anxiety attack, but I didn't know why. I wanted to cry, to scream at the top of my lungs, but why, why.

When I reached the parking area, Dr. Shannon was waiting in his car. He got out, and walked over and opened my door. I jumped out of the car, and grabbed him in a bear hug, like some kind of idiot. He pushed me to arm length to look into my eyes I could see my behavior alarmed him.

He managed to put a smile on his lips, then he said: "Suzanna, it's so nice to see you again, come let's go into the office, where we can be more comfortable."

When we got into the office, I burst into tears. He led me to a chair, and then left the room. He came back with a glass of water. He gave me the glass then he took a seat behind the desk, there he sat silently, waiting for me to get control of my emotions. I blew my nose, wiped away my tears, took a long swallow of water, and began:

"Dr. Shannon, I'm so sorry, I don't know why this is happening. I can't explain why I'm feeling this way; you've just got to help me, please."

"Okay, now Suzanna, you just wait until you are calm enough to talk, let's just sit quietly for a few more minutes, until you feel better." It seemed like hours before I finally got myself together. I drank most of the water, put the glass down, and managed a little smile before I spoke. "I think I'm ready to talk now, I just don't know what came over me. School has been fun.

I met a wonderful doctor to be, and we are the best of friends. His name is Tony, just before I came home, he wrote a letter and told me he loved me. He wanted to know if I felt the same. My problem is, I don't know if I love him or not."

"Is he pressuring you to tell him you love him?" asked Dr. Shannon.

"Oh, no, you see we know it will be four more years, before we could even think about marriage."

"I'm sorry, Suzanna, but I don't see any problem, just keep talking, and maybe I will understand."

"I guess I'm afraid he would be hurt, if I refused to have a relationship with him now."

"You mean a sexual relationship?"

"Yeah, I'm sure he doesn't think we should wait four years."

"How do you really feel about this, Suzanna?"

"That's just it, I don't want to have sex before marriage."

"Are you sure Tony will ask you to have a relationship?"

"I'm not positive he will, but isn't that how all men think about sex?"

"No, Suzanna, that isn't how all men think, you have the right to say no, even if he should ask you."

"You see, Dr. Shannon, we are the best of friends, and I would never deliberately hurt him."

"Now think about this Suzanna, if he is as good a friend as you think, your saying no won't change a thing."

"Do you honestly believe that in your heart, Dr. Shannon?"

"Yes, Suzanna, I do."

Driving home I was feeling better, but I still didn't have complete calmness within my being. I still felt a dark cloud hanging over me. I will see Janet before I leave. She can always make me feel better.

Thanksgiving day was busy, with cooking and eating all day. After supper I excused myself, claiming a headache. I knew if I spent much more time talking with Mother, she would sense something was bothering me. Then she would try to talk me into staying home for a while, until things were better. I had told her my talk with Dr. Shannon fixed everything. I can't bring myself to even mention Tony to my parents, I don't know why. I guess I just don't want the third degree from them. I've decided to visit Janet tomorrow, and maybe even go back to school on Saturday. Somehow I feel a need to see Tony, as soon as possible.

I came down to breakfast shortly after Daddy left for work, on Friday morning. Over breakfast with Mother, I told her I was gonna visit Janet today.

"I hope you understand my need to visit with Janet, Mother, she would never speak to me again, if I came home and didn't let her know."

"Sure, I understand, honey, just give me an idea when you will be home, in case I need to run an errand or something."

"Oh, I can be home by the time Daddy gets home, if that's okay with you."

"Sure, I will be expecting you here for supper, enjoy your visit, dear."

Mother never ceases to amaze me. I thought I might get a little resistance from her, about not having enough time with me. I wonder what she is so preoccupied with. It seems she was almost pleased that I wouldn't be home today, she actually seemed eager for me to leave. I will never understand Mother; we have always been strangers to each other. I wonder if every girl is as puzzled about her mother as I am.

I rang Janet's doorbell repeatedly, I had decided she wasn't home, but just as I turned to leave the door opened. Janet just stood there with her mouth hanging open, like she thought I was a ghost.

"Hello Janet," I said, waving my hand in front of her face.

"SUZANNA! I can't believe it's you, why didn't you tell me you were coming home for Thanksgiving? Come on in this house for goodness' sake," she held the door open wide.

After we were seated in the kitchen, she wanted to know what I wanted to drink.

"I'm so glad you are home, how long are you staying?" she asked while she was fixing our iced tea.

"I'm thinking about going back tomorrow."

"Tomorrow, how long have you been home, why didn't you call before now?"

"I came home Wednesday, but I have to be back for classes Monday."

"Then you don't have to go back until Sunday afternoon, do you?"

"Yes, I do, because there is someone I need to see on Sunday afternoon."

"'Uh-huh, so you have met someone, sounds important too."

"He is important, and a very good friend, but don't read any more than that into it, okay."

"Is it that Tony, you've wrote about?"

"Yeah, the one and the same, he only has one more year, then he will be going to Emory University for his internship. He's a wonderful person, but I'm afraid I've misled him. He wrote a letter, which I received the day before I left, confessing his love for me. We never have even embraced, or kissed, so you can imagine what a shock this was for me. I'm not sure of my feeling for him, but I can't allow myself to hurt him, Janet. I need someone to tell me what to do, I thought you might help me find the answer."

"Now Suzanna, here you go again, surely you had to do or say something to make him think you cared for him, so just think real hard, now what was it?"

"He said I didn't have to be in love with him now, that I would have at least four years to decide. I just can't keep his hopes up that

I might love him in time, if I'm not sure."

"Oh, my poor friend, I don't know how you manage to get yourself into these kind of situations. You are the luckiest person I know, everyone you meet falls in love with you, but you never know how you feel."

"Are you saying that you don't think I'm capable of loving anyone, is that what you are implying Janet?"

"Suzanna, all I know is, I can't tell you how you will feel, when you fall in love. You are the only one that will know when the right person comes along."

"So you are saying that if Tony is the right one, I will automatically know, without a doubt?"

"Yeah, that's pretty much what I'm saying I guess."

I decided it was time to change the subject, I could see Janet wasn't gonna be able to help me.

She sounded almost disgusted with me, and my problems.

"Where is "Little Bit", I'll bet she's growing like a weed?"

"She's visiting with Rick's parents. It's the first time she's been away this long, and I miss her terribly. I don't think I'm gonna let her go away for a whole week again, until she's in her teens."

"I can imagine how you must miss her. She's probably missing you too."

"I doubt if she misses me, she thinks she's grown now."

We had a pleasant afternoon together. I believe I noted a little tension with Janet, when I asked about Rick. Whatever was bothering her, she didn't open up to me the way she used to do. I know how much Janet's marriage means to her. I hope they aren't having problems. I will have to start writing to her more often, to give her a chance to confide in me. She seems a little depressed.

Chapter Twenty-Five

After supper, I told my parents I would be leaving the next afternoon. To my surprise, they didn't even question why I was leaving a day early. Maybe they are making a new life together, now that I'm out of the house. I sure hope that is what's going on.

When I arrived back at school, I sent Tony a note, asking him to meet me Sunday afternoon.

Ruth hadn't got back yet, so I had a long night of tossing and turning. This was my first night alone, in this big old Castle, as Ruth liked to call it. I know it's childish and silly, but I just couldn't relax until dawn. I had a monstrous headache. How in the world could I meet Tony this afternoon feeling like warmed over death?

I decided I would just skip church, and get some sleep, now the dark was gone. This will be my first time to miss church, since I have been here. Maybe no one will check my room this morning, since Ruth and I aren't expected back until tonight. However if the room is checked, and I am found here, it would mean a demerit for me. The school is very strict about going to church.

I awoke at noontime, and after my shower, I felt much better. It seemed a lifetime, before two o'clock arrived. I was a bit hungry, for I didn't dare go to lunch in the dinning room. After all I wasn't supposed to be here yet. I ate a snack of peanut butter crackers, and went on down to meet the bus. It will be just awful, if he didn't get my message in time.

Tony stepped off the bus, with his wonderful warm smile, and I felt my heart flutter in my chest. He grabbed me in a bear hug, and kissed me on top of my head. He took my hand is his, and led me down a tree shaded path.

"Suzanna I've missed you so much how was your visit?"

"My visit was miserable, thank you, but you couldn't have missed me, because we haven't even missed one date."

"I knew you were far away from me though, that's why I missed you."

"Not far Tony, only about two hours drive, and you could have gone with me, you know."

He stepped in front of me and stopped. Our eyes met, he leaned toward me, and gently kissed my lips. He held me close for a moment, and then stepped away, to look at me. I opened my mouth to say, "I don't know what," but he interrupted. "Shush, you don't have to explain, we have plenty of time." I felt the tears fill my eyes, and my lips trembled. He drew me into his arms, so gently. I have no idea how long we stood there, I don't think either of us ever wanted to move away from each other again. I felt so safe, but I also felt like my heart would burst, with sorrow.

Do I have something missing inside, I wonder. Why can't I feel the same way Tony does. He deserves a lot better than me, this I know for sure.

I finally pulled away, and softly whispered, "I'm sorry if I have caused you pain, or misled you, you've got to believe me, Tony. I would never hurt you on purpose, never."

"Sure I know that, so don't worry your pretty little head about it. Let's just let time tell, and in the meantime, we are best friends okay? I'm not asking you to commit to anything." When I started to say something, he put his hand over my mouth, no, no more talk about this now," he said. We strolled along the walk, hand in hand, and Tony carried the conversation as though nothing out of the ordinary had happened. It was a stressful time for me, for my heart was heavy with guilt feelings Tony was laughing and talking, like old times, and I finally relaxed and felt more like myself again. When we went to meet the bus, he bent and kissed me on the forehead, as he had done so many times before.

"I'll see you again next Sunday," he said, and stepped up into the bus.

"Sure," I answered, and waved goodbye.

When I got back to the dorm, Ruth was settling in from her trip home. I told her all about the afternoon with Tony.

"I'll say one thing Suzanna, I can't in all my dreams, understand how anyone could have second thoughts, about loving someone like Tony. I would do anything to have what you have with him, and I do mean anything."

"Ruth, please don't rub it in, I know how lucky I am, to have a friend like Tony, but I have to be sure about love. No matter how nice and understanding he might be, maybe perfect even.

When I commit myself to marriage, I intend it to last for the rest of my life. You know, and I know, it wouldn't be easy to be married to a doctor."

"Look at it this way, Suzanna, you could have your own mansion, you could afford the finest clothes, you could give big dinner parties, you could afford to have a nanny for your children, why I could go on and on."

"Sure, you are right, I could have all money could buy, but how often would I have the presence of my husband?"

"Good grief Suzanna, you surely don't think marriage is one long honeymoon. Why after a year or so, you probably won't care if you have much time with him or not."

"That's not the way I believe marriage should be Ruth, so I'll just say goodnight, now if you don't mind, I need some rest."

While I was drifting off to sleep, the things that Ruth had said meandered through my mind.

Could she be right that after a while, one would get tired of the husband being around all the time? I don't hardly think so, but when I visited Janet last week, I'm not sure that she wasn't getting a bit tired of marriage. I think I'll call Janet tomorrow, and give her a chance to confide in me, I have this gut feeling something is bothering her, and as always I had to tell all my troubles, and didn't give her a chance to talk about hers. I sure haven't kept my promise to myself that I would stop being self-centered.

The next evening between classes, I went to the office to call Janet. When she answered, I couldn't be sure if it was her or not.

"Hello, is this Janet?"

"Yeah, this is Janet, is that you Suzanna?"

"It's me, I didn't wake you I hope you sound kinda groggy?"

"I lay down for a few minutes, I guess I dozed off, is something wrong Suzanna?"

"No, nothing's wrong, I just thought I'd call and see how things are with you. When I was home, you didn't quite seem like yourself to me. As usual, I went on and on about my problems, and didn't give you a chance to talk about yours."

"Suzanna, you never cease to amaze me, how in this world did you know that I needed to talk to you?"

"I have a couple of things, are you sure you have the time, and that you want to hear them?"

"Of course, Janet, I wouldn't have called if I didn't want to know, now tell me what is wrong."

"Okay, here goes. First thing, I'm pregnant, and I'm feeling lousy, that's why you caught me asleep in the middle of the day."

"Oh, that's great, you wanted a boy, and "Little Bit" is two now, isn't she? I remember you telling me that two years apart was about right for them to grow up being close to each other."

"I might have said that, but that's not what's bothering me really."

"Then tell me what's so wrong that you are not happy about having another baby."

"It's Ricky, he is drinking every night, and he has been drunk the last two weekends. I've tried to talk with him, but he gets angry and walks out."

"Does he know you are pregnant?"

"No, I haven't told him. I'm afraid that might make him drink even more."

"No, Janet, I don't agree, I think that might give him something to look forward to, you know he loves babies as much as you do. I'm sure every man wants a son. This might give him enough reason to stop his drinking."

"Maybe, but what if it's not a boy?"

"I don't think that would matter at all with Rick, look how crazy he is about "Little Bit" another daughter would be just fine. How far along are you Janet?"

"Oh, I haven't been to the doctor yet."

"You tell Rick tonight at the supper table, before he has time to start drinking, and if I know him as well as I think I do, he will be happy about the baby."

"You know, you are probably right, Suzanna."

"Sure I am. My next class is getting close, so I'm gonna have to say bye for now. If you need to talk to me in more detail, I'll call you again the same time tomorrow."

"Oh, no, that's not necessary; I'll just write you a letter and let you know how things are going. I feel a lot better already, thanks for calling Suzanna."

I walked to my next class, wondering what could have happened in Janet's marriage, to cause Rick to start drinking in excess. He had always had a beer after supper to relax, but he had never been drunk before, not to my knowledge. Janet had been so happy until now. Maybe Ruth is right after all, after a couple of years the new wears off. I wonder what advice Janet would have given me about getting married, if I had asked her today. She sounded so hurt with Rick, I dare to doubt that their marriage will ever be the same after this. A few days later I received a letter from Janet.

Dear Suzanna,

You don't know what a life-saver you've been, by calling me the other day. You can't imagine how low I felt before you called. I took your advice, and you were absolutely right about Rick. He was so happy, about the baby, that he didn't drink, not one beer after supper. I've had his supper on the table every day, and he has been home on time every day. It's almost like we were, in the beginning of our marriage. He's been so attentive, I can hardly believe it.

I'm gonna be truthful with you. Divorce had entered my mind, before I knew I was pregnant.

Once I knew I was pregnant, I felt doomed. I have to admit also that I haven't been that good a wife, for a while now. I didn't have supper fixed every night, and I was hateful and grumpy most of the time.

I'm feeling a lot better, but of course that's because my life is better. I didn't realize how uptight I was, until things started getting back to normal. I think I might understand now, about how a person could contemplate taking their own life. I'm sorry if I wasn't very understanding about your suicide attempt. I just hadn't been that depressed before.

You will never know the favor you did me, by calling me when you did. You threw out the lifeline to me, and I'm so sorry I didn't do the same for you, when you needed it. When

I start trying to tell you how to live your life again, I hope you will be strong and tell me to butt-out.

Dear friend, I will never try to sell you on marriage again. Don't read me wrong, I still love Ricky dearly, but he has disappointed me a few times more than I ever expected. However I know I haven't been a perfect partner myself. I don't think marriage is for everyone anymore. It's like I've heard all my life, it's a give and take thing, and it usually is mostly giving. I think the woman does the most giving, just to keep peace in the relationship. As you know there aren't that many selfless people in the world. No I'm not saying, I'm one of the selfless, you know me better than that. I guess life would be dull without disagreements occasionally. My dear friend I have bored you long enough, so I will close. I know you don't have a lot of time to write, so just call me whenever you get the time between classes.

As ever your best friend,
Janet

I am so glad to hear the good news from Janet, now I can focus on my studies again. Knowing that Janet was so unhappy made it hard to concentrate in class. I hope my grades don't drop this semester, because of my concern. Tony has noticed I don't always hear what he is saying. He asked me several times what's bothering me, but I don't think it would be fair to burden him with my worries. My excuse to him has been that I am extra tired lately. His advice is that I should get more sleep and rest. Naturally he would say that, since he plans to be a doctor. He is such a considerate person.

Chapter Twenty-Six

Christmas holidays are almost here, and I can't believe how fast time has passed. Tony will be going home also. Just one more semester, and he will be leaving for medical school. I wonder if distance will make a difference in the way I feel about our friendship. I admit there are times, when I feel so close to him, but what proof do I have that this closeness is love. True and lasting love. I hope I will know for sure before he leaves.

I can't depend on Janet's help in deciding, because she isn't sure about her own feelings right now. I feel odd talking to Ruth about it, because she still has a crush on Tony. As far as Ruth is concerned, he's some kind of hero or god. So she would tell me I am ungrateful, and possibly a little crazy, not to be in love with Tony. I really dread being home for two whole weeks, but Mother is beside herself with joy, our having such a long visit ahead.

I'm waiting on the bus for our last Sunday together, before the holiday begins. Realizing it will be so long before we see each other again, gives me an empty feeling. This must mean I feel more than friendship for Tony. How will I ever know for sure? Tony took my hand as I stood up. I squeezed his hand lightly. He stopped to face me, took my other hand in his and said: "Goodness, do I detect some new feeling in my forever friend?"

"Why, I don't know what you mean, sir," I said, smiling at him.

"Oh, but yes you do, don't give me that innocent treatment of yours."

"I'm confused Tony, I've been thinking about how soon you will be leaving, for medical school."

"How do you feel about me leaving, Suzanna?"

"I feel lonely and you are not even gone, but I don't understand exactly why."

"Have you thought maybe you are possibly just a little bit in love with me?" he teased.

"That thought has crossed my mind, but how can I be sure?"

"Oh Suzanna, my sweet Suzanna, there are no guarantees in love, you just have to be willing to give it a chance, and if it is love, it will grow."

"How do you know for sure that you love me, Tony?"

"I can't put my feelings in words. I just know in my heart that my world won't be complete without you. Just quit worrying over this. I think time will tell for sure, and maybe while we are apart for these two weeks, you will know, without a doubt."

He pulled me close and held me for just a moment, and then he gently released me and gazed deep into my eyes. I could see and feel love radiating from him. I was frightened, because I knew I would have to confess my past to him, before we could carry our friendship any further. He deserved to know that I am not the purest of virgins. I just couldn't bring myself to tell him, not just yet. I will tell him everything when we get back from the Christmas holidays

If only I hadn't been so eager to grow up, I wouldn't be in this situation. I believe I might really be falling in love with Tony. I'm just not sure he would feel the same love for me, if he knew about my past. Why had I been so strong willed, and why hadn't I listened to Daddy about Fred. How many more times in my life would these words come back to haunt me? "If you go out with Fred, you will be sorry," those were Daddy's exact words.

When we were waiting for Tony's bus, neither of us was talking. We stood holding hands and gazing into each other's eyes. It was as if we were mesmerized. The bus arrived, but instead of being among the first on as always before Tony waited until the last. Just before he stepped up on the bus, he bent down and gently kissed my lips, he whispered, "I love you." When he was seated on the bus, I ran to his window, and blew him a kiss, and mouthed those three little words back to him "I love you." I felt the warm tears run down my cheeks, walking back to my dorm.

It was morning and I was finally on my way home, but I felt no excitement whatsoever. I felt a part of me was missing, just knowing how long it would be before I would see Tony again. I didn't know how I would tell Mother and Daddy about Tony; I only knew that I had to find a way somehow.

When I arrived home, you would have thought Mother hadn't seen me in years, the way she carried on.

"My goodness, you are looking more beautiful than ever. There is a glow about you now dear. I'll just bet you have met someone special," said Mother, while we climbed the stairs to my room.

I was so glad Mother opened the subject that I could have hugged her right then and there. I wonder sometimes if Mother can read my mind, it surely seems that way. "Mother, I have met someone special, but I don't know how you could tell, just by looking at me."

"Oh honey, love always shows in the eyes, you are in love aren't you? What's his name, and when can we meet him?

"Hey, Mother wait a minute, we have two whole weeks, that will give you plenty of time for the third degree," I laughed.

"Oh, at least tell me his name, and that he is handsome."

"His name is Tony, he is very handsome, and he's studying to be a doctor."

"Oh, Suzanna, a doctor, I'm so happy for you. I will never have to worry about your well-being again. When do you plan to be married?"

"Oh, that will be at least four years from now, after this next semester, he will be going to Emory University. As you know Mother, it takes a long time to become a doctor, therefore we haven't even given marriage a thought yet."

"With our help, you could get married before he finishes school, you know we could always help you financially."

"Thanks, but no thanks, Mother, the thought is sweet, but when and if we get married, we will be completely on our own. I want to finish my education also, so we have plenty of time to plan our wedding. Tony is a strong and independent person, and he would never accept financial help from his folks, much less mine.

The days went by and Mother and I talked about Tony more than anything else. Mother had endless questions, and even wanted to know his favorite food. It was then I realized how little I knew about Tony's personal preferences. After all we had never had a date outside the campus.

My mother's questions brought the facts home to me. I really didn't know Tony as well as I had thought. I didn't know anything about his family. I assume they are middle class. All of a sudden it dawned on me, how few facts I actually knew about Tony. Why had

146

I been considering spending the rest of my life with a stranger? I do miss him so much, but I missed seeing Janet an awful lot when I first went off to school too. So it could be his friendship I miss, I might not be in love at all.

I only found time to visit Janet once, while I was home. I didn't ever bring up my confused life at all; Janet needed me to listen to her problems for a change. I am concerned about Janet. It's the first time I have seen her so depressed. I feel she needs to see a professional. Janet hadn't wanted another baby right now, so I hope that's why she is depressed. I didn't see the closeness with Rick and Janet that they had when I left for college. Janet told me Rick had quit drinking, but I'm not sure that's the truth. Somehow, Rick is not the same toward me either. Janet tried to reassure me that when her pregnancy got a little further along, she would be her old self again. She said not to worry about her, that's easier said than done.

Chapter Twenty-Seven

The morning I left to go back to school was hectic; Mother wanted me to wait until after lunch to head back. I just couldn't wait that long, I needed to see Tony as soon as possible. I missed Ruth also, and I couldn't wait to hear about her holiday. I finally got away around ten o'clock, with the car loaded with cookies, cake and candy that Mother insisted I take.

I finally arrived back at school. Ruth was already there. She helped me unload the car, while she talked a blue streak, about all her cousins. It seemed she had dozens of them, and of course she had to tell me what was happening in each one of their lives, as if I were interested. Don't get me wrong, I think the world of Ruth, but sometimes I can hardly tolerate her. She's a person who can just go on and on about the very same subject, like the old saying, beating a dead horse. I hardly ever mentioned Janet to Ruth, because I sense a little jealously on her part. I defiantly don't talk about Tony to Ruth anymore, because I know there is jealously there for sure. So most of the time I do the listening in our friendship.

Ruth is so caught up in her own life she doesn't notice that she does all the talking. This is just the way I used to treat Janet, so I guess it's pay back time for me. Poor Janet how did she tolerate me all those years. Sunday has finally arrived, and I'm anxious to get to the bus stop, to meet Tony. I don't think I can eat a bite of lunch. It seems a lifetime since I last saw Tony. When lunch was finally over, I was one of the first to run for the bus stop. I stood close to the bus door while the guys got off, hoping to see Tony's face before he saw me. Then the bus was empty, but Tony wasn't among the crowd. I looked all around at each face, wondering how I could have missed him. Then I had this sick feeling, maybe Tony doesn't want to see me anymore. I started to walk away, and then I felt a hand touch my shoulder. I turned, expecting to see Tony, thinking he had pulled a trick on me, and had been hiding in the crowd. The face I saw was a stranger, I felt my smile fade on my lips.

"Hello. My name is James, are you Suzanna Stoggins?"

"Yes, I am Suzanna, but I don't know you, I am here to meet Tony Bryson, do you by chance know Tony?"

He took my hand and led me toward one of the benches, "Let's sit down while I tell you why I am here."

I began to tremble as I followed him to the bench, I sat down, then I looked up at him and asked, "Who sent you, and what did you come to tell me?"

"To be honest, I drew the short straw, and that's why I came to tell you. All of Tony's friends got together, and none of us wanted to be the one to tell you. We knew how much you meant to him, and that one of us would have to bring the news. You see, Tony died in a car accident over the holidays, and none of us knew how to get in touch with you."

I felt my body slip off the bench onto the ground. When I awoke, James was kneeling beside me with a wet handkerchief held to my brow. Tears were tracking down his cheeks when he said, "I'm so sorry, I just didn't know any other way to tell you; now you tell me what I can do for you to help you."

I got to my feet very slowly, with his help. I took a deep breath, and looked at him, and answered, "There was no other way for you to tell me, I want to thank you for coming, otherwise I might not have ever known what happened. Do you know if it was instant, or did he have to suffer?"

"They said he was dead at the scene, so thank goodness, he didn't have to suffer."

"I guess he never got around to telling his folks about me. You see Tony knew how to call me, if he needed to, and if his parents had known about me, surely they would have let me know."

"Tony hadn't told his parents about you, because he knew they would get upset, if they ever learned how much you meant to him."

"Why," I asked, "how do you know this?"

"His mother was so set on him being a doctor that she wouldn't even think about him having a girlfriend. That's why she sent him way down here to this college, where the guys are five miles away from the girls. This way she was hoping he would never have the chance to meet a girl.

"What was she gonna do about girls when he went to Emory?"

149

"I don't know, but knowing his mother, I can tell you she would have thought of something, you can bet on that."

"Then I guess I didn't miss a thing by never meeting his parents."

"Oh, you would have liked his dad; Tony was a lot like him, in ways and looks."

I feel like a part of me is dying, I just have to be alone, I hope James will understand, it was so humane of him to come to tell me. So I said to him, "James I do thank you so much, for coming to tell me, but I'm gonna have to go back to my dorm now."

"Sure I understand, I'm glad I got to meet you, you are just as nice as Tony said, I can see how he fell in love with you."

"Thank you, you are so kind," I said, and I walked away, the tears washing down my face. I was so thankful Ruth was out when I got to our room. I lay across my bed and cried until there were no more tears. I was go glad that Tony didn't suffer, and I was also glad that he felt I would eventually fall in love with him. Thank goodness I had waited to tell him about my past mistakes.

I must have loved him, because I feel my heart breaking. Why did something bad happen to everyone I care about? Tony would have made such a companionate doctor. He was so caring and gentle. Why do the best people in the world, have to die so young?

When Ruth came in and I told her, she cried right along with me. When time came to go to the dinning hall, she told me that she would explain about Tony, and bring me back a tray to our room. This was a blessing to me, for I didn't think I could face anyone else today. For Ruth's kindness I would try to eat my supper, although I couldn't stand the thought of food right now.

On Monday, I called Janet. I told her about Tony. I hesitated to tell her, because she wasn't in the greatest frame of mind either. However, I had to talk to someone, and I knew Mother would insist I come home for a while. Janet told me I should come home right away. I told her I was going to finish the year before coming home that I had to go on with my dream of being a teacher, because that would be what Tony would want me to do.

"Suzanna, are you sure you will be okay?"

"Yeah," I said, "I want you to promise me you are going to be okay also."

"Sure I will. I'm already beginning to bounce back to normal, since I started my vitamins. I'm not having morning sickness anymore, so I can start pigging-out. You know how I enjoy eating when I'm pregnant. By the time you see me again, I'll be glowing in good health. I wish I could take some of your pain; I'm so sorry this has happened to you, please take care of yourself."

"I will, Janet, I have to go to my next class now, so good-bye until next time."

Walking to my next class, I searched my mind for a way to tell my parents. I know they will insist I come home to heal, but that's the last thing I want to do. I'm going to put all, my mind into my studies, and get my diploma as soon as possible. I know the sooner I get on with my life, the better. I learned that from Lucy's death. I hope I can explain this to Mother and Daddy, so they can be at ease with my plan to stay on here in school. I think it best to tell them in a letter, rather than by phone. This way there won't be a debate.

Chapter Twenty-Eight

This semester is taking forever, the time just drags on. No matter how much or how hard I study, I can't get the pain to go away. It's almost time for Janet to have her baby, so I've decided to go home for the summer after all. I simply can't stay here and study all summer, now that Tony is gone. This decision will make my folks happy, as well as Janet.

The day finally came for summer vacation, and I can't wait to get on the road. The trip wasn't long, my thoughts on the way got me there much quicker than I expected. Mother was overjoyed to have me home again. She acted as though I had been away for years, and insisted in helping me settle into my old room again.

"Oh, honey, I'm so happy you decided to come home for the summer. We are going to go out and do things together this summer, just the two of us, I'm so excited just thinking about it."

"What exactly are you saying, Mother?"

"Your daddy is working a lot of overtime, expanding the business, and that will leave us a lot more time to spend with each other, just you and me. Don't you think that will be fun, like when you were small?"

"Mother, you know it's almost time for Janet to have her baby, and I plan to help her as much as possible."

"Suzanna, you don't owe all your time to Janet. We can just pay someone to help her."

"Mother, why can't you understand, I want to help her. Hiring a stranger wouldn't be the same. I want to give my time to her as her best friend. She wouldn't allow me to hire someone to help her, in the first place."

"You are right, dear, I don't understand, you have always preferred to be with your friend, rather than me."

"Now Mother, you know it's not the same with you and me, as with Janet and me. She has been my best friend since second grade, she's the sister I never had."

"I'm sorry we couldn't give you a sister, it wasn't because we didn't try."

"I know, Mother, I'm not trying to make you feel guilty, I'm just trying to make you understand. Please, I don't want to hurt your feelings, there will still be time for us to do things together this summer, okay?"

Mother looked bewildered, she started to leave the room. When she reached the door, she turned and said: "Okay honey, the invitation is open; anytime you feel the need to spend some time with me. I want you to know, I'll always be here for you."

I rang the bell, and gave my special little knock. Janet knew right away that it was me, and she opened the door, her arms open wide.

"Suzanna, you don't know how glad I am, you decided to come home for the summer." She hugged me tightly. I backed away to look at her, and just couldn't hold my tongue.

"My goodness, Janet, you are as big as a whale, when did you say this baby is due?"

"Oh, any day now," she laughed. "Yes I am big as a whale, I've gained forty pounds this time. Poor "Little Bit" can hardly find enough lap to sit on anymore. I don't dare sit on the sofa when there is no one here to help me get up."

"Where is my little godchild, anyway?"

"She's down for her nap, she's only been asleep about ten minutes so we will have time to talk without interruption. Come on to our favorite place, (the kitchen table) and we will get something to drink."

I couldn't help but notice how tired Janet looked. I don't remember her looking this bad when she was carrying "Little Bit". She also looks so unhappy. I don't believe everything is as good as she says it is.

"Okay, Suzanna, how are you dealing with things now, and be honest with me."

"I'm as okay as I will ever be, but you know things won't ever be the same again, however I'm reconciling to that fact. What I want to know is how are you really feeling Janet? You seem worn out, are you not getting enough rest or what? I remember you were beautiful when you were pregnant with little Jane. You were glowing with happiness."

"I am tired, but after all it's impossible to get comfortable enough to rest the last few weeks.

The second pregnancy isn't as easy or exciting as the first. You know what's ahead when time comes."

"Are you saying you don't want this baby?"

"That's not it, but you know I also have the little two year old, to take care of now. Jane is out of one thing into two, and it gets tough at times to keep up with her. I know all this extra weight ain't good either, to be honest, but enough about me, what have you been doing to get yourself back together?"

"Let's say I have the best grades probably in the entire school. I use all my time studying to keep from thinking.

Right after Tony's accident I thought I would just finish all my schooling, before I came back home. Then it wasn't long before I realized, I just couldn't hold out mentally or physically. I need a break, and I need some time with you and my parents. I'm still full of guilt, because I wasn't completely honest with Tony. I'm not sure I'll ever know what love really is. I know without Tony in my life, I will always have an empty place in my heart. That doesn't mean that I was in love with him though, because I will always have a place for Lucy in my heart too.

"I don't know, sometimes I don't think I know what true love is anymore either," answered Janet.

"Rick hasn't really quit drinking, has he, Janet?"

Janet's shoulders began to shake, as she started to cry. I sat quietly, as she let her emotions flow. After what seemed forever, she didn't have anymore, tears she wiped her face with the wet washcloth I handed her and began:

"No, Ricky hasn't quit drinking. He stopped for a while; now when he comes home from work, he eats his supper, goes to the fridge, gets his first beer, and heads for the couch and the TV. Sometimes he drinks a whole six-pack before he comes to bed. He works everyday, but we never talk anymore. It's hard to tell if he wants this baby or not. He has become a stranger to me.

I really don't know what's gonna happen with us. After the baby is born, if things don't change, I guess our marriage will be over."

"No, Janet, don't think that way. You can't just throw away all your years of happiness, and you can't take away your children's father. You and Rick will have to go to a marriage counselor, and try to fix things."

"Suzanna, we don't have the money for a marriage counselor?"

"You don't have to have money, the county has free counseling for those who can't afford to pay."

"Are you sure, Suzanna?"

"Yeah I'm sure. Lucy told me a friend of hers got help from the county. She said if her friend hadn't got help, she believed she would have killed herself, because she was so depressed. They helped her and her husband work out their problems, and they are still together, at least they were at the time Lucy told me about it."

"Oh, I'm so glad to hear this, I have been thinking that things were hopeless for us, but now you have given me hope again."

"Janet, you must never give up hope, I have learned that first hand. You and Rick will turn things around. I know you two were in love when you got married, so you can find that love again. Being happily married has always been your dream. I know you well enough to know that you of all people will never give up your dream."

"I hope you are right, Suzanna, if you're not I don't know what I will do. Having to raise two kids alone frightens me more than you know. I'm just not the kind of woman who wants to work outside the home. I don't have training for any kind of vocation, since I've never been interested in a career. I know for certain that I don't want to go on welfare."

After I was in bed that night, I tried to imagine what terrible thing could have happened to Janet's marriage. I couldn't comprehend how so much love and devotion could just disappear. I know how strong Janet's love has been, and she has never had any doubt that her happiness with Rick wouldn't last forever. This simply can't be the end of their marriage. After the baby comes everything will be okay, it just has to be.

Chapter Twenty-Nine

It seemed I had just fallen asleep, when my phone woke me. It was Rick calling to tell me he had a son.

"Oh, Rick, I'm so happy it's over, is Janet okay?"

"Yeah, she and little Joseph are both doing fine. He's a big one all right; he weighed eight pound and three ounces."

"Good grief, are you sure Janet is all right? I'm so glad it is a boy, now you have someone to carry on your name huh, and someone to watch the sports on TV with you too."

"Yeah, it is good to have a son I guess, but that really wasn't the important thing. I just wanted it to be healthy.

"You be sure and tell Janet I'll be over to see her tomorrow, and congratulations to you Rick."

"Sure will, bye now Suzanna."

I'll bet that is why Janet got so emotional yesterday, because it was so close to time for the baby. These thoughts were running through my mind, when I fell back into slumber land.

I could hardly wait to go to the hospital the next morning I was trying to contain myself, because I didn't want to get there too early, after all Janet needed to rest. I finally decided I might as well go on down for breakfast, I would try to take longer than usual to eat, to allow more time to pass. As always, Mother was in the kitchen.

"Good morning you are up rather early," she said.

"Uh-huh, Janet had her baby last night, and I can't wait to see him."

"I thought I heard your phone ring kinda late last night."

"I think it was around two or two thirty this morning, Mother."

"So it was a boy, give Janet my congratulations."

"He weighted over eight pounds, they named him Joseph. I love that name, don't you?"

"Yes, that is a good strong name," said mother.

I stopped at the gift shop to get Janet and Joseph a gift. While I was paying for my purchase, I was aware someone walked up behind me in line. Never in a hundred years would I have thought it was someone I knew. When I turned to leave, our eyes met. I was so surprised I blurted out:

"My goodness Bill, what are you doing here?" I couldn't believe how hard my heart was pounding. I hoped he couldn't see my blouse moving, that's how strong my heartbeat felt, I could even feel it in my throat, as if I might choke.

"Suzanna, it's been so long since I've seen you, this is such a surprise. Rick told me you went away to college. How are things going with you?"

"Yes, I have been away, but decided to take the summer off. I'm enjoying school; I don't know why I put it off so long. I came to see Rick's and Janet's little son." I quickly glanced at his ring finger, while asking him if he had someone in the hospital. Good there is no ring, but did that really mean anything, some married men don't wear wedding rings. I hope he didn't notice me looking at his hand, with that thought I felt my face flush, and I instantly felt like a fool.

"Yes, my mother had to have her gall bladder out, and I came by to check on her."

"I do hope she will be better soon," I said, heading for the elevator. Bill walked along with me, and when the elevator stopped, he got on too. I pressed the third floor, and asked him what floor he wanted. "Two please," he answered. We stood completely silent while the elevator started up. When we stopped on two, Bill stepped off. Other people were getting on, thank goodness, and this made things less awkward for both of us. Bill smiled and casually waved goodbye, and said: "See you around, Suzanna."

I was completely breathless, when I finally reached Janet's room. I felt like one could light a match on my cheeks.

"Hello, it's about time you got here. I had about given up on you," said Janet.

"You know me better than that, I felt I should give you a little time to rest, before you saw my face and had to listen to this mouth," I laughed.

"Oh, what beautiful flowers, thanks Suzanna, they are probably the only ones I'll get you know."

"Come on now, you know Rick will bring you roses tonight, is he working today?"

"Yeah, you know we can't afford to miss a whole day's pay, not on our pitiful budget."

"How are you feeling, now the baby is here?"

"How do you think you would feel Suzanna, if you had just had an eight pound baby?"

"You want the truth, it sounds awful painful to me, Janet. Where is the nursery, I want to see my new godchild?"

"Okay, give me a minute, and I will walk down with you, I want to see him again too."

On our way I casually mentioned that I ran into Bill in the gift shop.

"You saw Bill Norton here? He's not married now is he? Did you talk with him, who does he know in the hospital?"

"I don't know if he's married, he wasn't wearing a wedding band. His mother is here, she had an operation, and she's doing fine. We didn't talk that much really. He was as lost for words as I was and his face flushed a few times, just like mine did. I felt so strange just being near him, I wish I could remember what happened, if anything, the last time we were together. I wish I had the chance to go back before the shock treatments. If I had only known how blank my past would become, I would have at least written a journal before the treatments."

"How did you feel when you saw him, explain it to me," said Janet.

"I thought my heart would pound right out of my chest. It beat so strong I thought he might hear it, or at least see my blouse moving."

"Doesn't it tell you anything, when you felt so much, just seeing Bill. Suzanna you must have been in love with him. You need to try your best to remember before the shock."

"Oh, Janet, you don't know how hard I've tried to remember, maybe someday it will all come back."

Little Joseph was a beautiful baby. We stood quietly admiring the perfect job that nature had done, with all the little ones in the nursery. On our way back to Janet's room she asked me if Bill asked to see me again.

"No, of course not, when he left the elevator, he just said, see you around and waved."

"Do you think he was glad to see you?"

"I don't know. I was too busy trying to hide how glad I was to see him."

"Why in heavens name would you want to hide the way you feel, Suzanna?"

"I need to know how a person feels about me first, and other than his occasional blushing, I couldn't read his feelings."

"Suzanna, what do you think his blushing could mean?"

"Maybe he was embarrassed. It might be different if I could remember what happened between us, can't you see what I mean, Janet?"

"Sure I can, I've already told you what a good time you had. I've told you all the things you told me about your relationship. Can't you remember just a little about the weekend you kept "Little Bit" for Rick and me when we went to Atlanta? You told me he stayed over Saturday night, and slept on the sofa. You said he was a perfect gentleman, and he would make some lucky girl a good husband. Do you know why you won't let these memories come back?"

"I don't know, unless something bad happened that night. Dr. Shannon told me not to try to bring back the past. The shock was to get rid of my past, at least the things that were making me sick. I'd best be going before the nurses ask me to leave. Your lunch will soon be here, I hope I haven't tired you out staying so long."

"No, you didn't tire me, I'm so glad you came. When will I see you again?"

"I don't know, if I don't get back to the hospital, call me when you get home. I want to come over and help you for a while, the way I did with "Little Bit", but of course I will go home in the evenings."

"You know you are welcome to stay over in the evenings, if you don't mind sleeping on the sofa."

"I know I'm welcome, but things could get crowded now, with two little ones. I would feel like I was imposing, which I didn't give a thought about when little Jane was born. Just mark it down that I've grown some in the last two years, for the better hopefully."

"You most certainly have grown, Suzanna. You do what is most comfortable for you, but always remember, you are welcome in our home."

I left the hospital hoping I might see Bill again. I knew the stirring in my heart when I saw Bill had to be more than just friendship. When he spoke, I felt a warmth go all through my whole body. This was a feeling I had never experienced before, not even with Tony. There will always be a place in my heart for Tony, but I know the feeling for Bill is different.

Chapter Thirty

Bill had left the hospital after a brief visit with his mother, because he had to go to work for the day. When lunchtime came he headed for the cafeteria, since he hadn't taken time to fix a lunch. Rick saw Bill, and motioned for him to join him, at his table. Bill took a seat across from Rick.

"I heard you have a brand new baby boy today," said Bill.

"Yeah, man, but how did you know?"

"I ran into Suzanna in the hospital this morning, and she told me."

"What were you doing at the hospital Bill, you are not sick I hope."

"Oh, no, Mother had her gall bladder out, and I dropped in to see her for a minute."

"So you talked with Suzanna. Did you two start up your friendship again by chance?"

"We both were kinda lost for words, I guess you might say. Do you think she would consider going out with me again Rick, or should I just try to forget her completely?"

"Man, if you haven't already forgotten her, I don't know if you can. The only way you will ever know if she will go out with you is to ask her. I know that's easier said than done, but that's the only thing I can tell you."

"I guess you are right, Rick, but I was thinking maybe you could run it by Janet, and maybe she could give you a clue. She could find out how Suzanna feels about us getting back together."

"Bill I felt bad when Suzanna hurt you before, and I told Janet, we would never play Cupid again, you sure you want me to do this?"

"Rick, I have to know how she feels about me. We had a fight the last time we were together.

She was so angry that I couldn't reason with her. I need to explain some things, and at least have a chance to part as friends even if there can never be a reconciliation. No matter what happens, I won't hold you or Janet responsible."

"Okay, buddy, if you are sure this is what you want, I'll get with Janet right away, this will make her jump with joy, all I ever hear from her is that Bill and Suzanna were meant for each other. She'll be thrilled to get another chance to get y'all together again."

After Bill went back to work that afternoon, he had to wonder if he was doing the right thing. He didn't want to feel the pain again, but he had to try one more time to win Suzanna. He knew he would never love anyone else the way he loved her. If it didn't work this time, he would close this chapter of his life forever.

Rick picked up a dozen roses in the gift shop, and then caught the elevator up to Janet's room. He could tell by the expression on Janet's face that the roses were a wonderful surprise for her.

"Oh, Ricky, the roses are so beautiful, but are you sure we can afford them?" Rick bent over the bed and kissed her, and then he said, "You don't worry about whether we can afford these roses, because you are worth the cost. You have just given me my first son, and I know it wasn't an easy job. I'm going to be the husband you deserve from now on. No more drinking every day.

I've got to be a good example for my son, and I'm starting right now.

"Oh, Ricky," she sobbed, "You don't know how happy this makes me, to hear those words. I've been so afraid that I might have to raise the kids alone. I know I haven't been the best wife at times, but I promise I will try harder. We used to be so happy, if we both give it our best, we can be that happy again, I just know we can."

"Yes we can my love, now let's go down and visit our son. Here let me help you with your slippers," he answered. They stood admiring little Joseph, as they held hands, for the first time in goodness knows when. Janet couldn't remember the last time she felt so loved and secure.

They strolled happily back to her room, when he had her settled back in bed, he took the chair beside the bed. His first words was: "Hon, I'll bet you can't guess who I ate lunch with today?"

"I have no idea, who?"

"Bill Norton, he doesn't usually buy his lunch like myself, but today he ate in the cafeteria. I was sitting alone so I invited him to join me. The first thing he said was that he saw Suzanna this morning when she came to visit with you. You are not going to believe this, but he asked me to ask you to find out if Suzanna would go out with him again. At first I said I didn't want to get involved, then I took one look at him and reconsidered. You know, honey, I believe Bill is in love with Suzanna, but don't you dare tell her I told you."

"Oh, Ricky, this is such exciting news, the meeting this morning shook Suzanna up too. When she told me about it, she tried to be nonchalant about the whole thing, but you know how she is. I think she's in love with Bill too, and I also believe deep inside her heart, she knows she loves him. For some unknown reason to me, she is afraid of love. I just hope she won't stay in denial until it's too late. My next visit with her, I will feel her out about Bill. I promise I won't say a word about what you have told me." Janet was happier than she had been in months. She was afraid she might have trouble falling asleep, after Rick left, and had decided she would ask for a sleeping pill, but she knew she wouldn't need it after all now, her world was at peace again.

She and little Joseph would be going home tomorrow.

Bill was disappointed when he couldn't locate Rick at lunch. Asking around, he was told Rick was off work, to take his wife and baby home from the hospital. Bill had gone back to the hospital the evening before, in hopes to see Suzanna again. Now he knew why Suzanna wasn't there, she would visit Janet at home today. He hoped Rick wouldn't forget to talk to Janet, about what they had discussed. He couldn't stand the suspense much longer; he had to know if he had a chance to win Suzanna back.

Chapter Thirty-One

I didn't go over to Janet's the day they came home, I felt the family needed time together to become acquainted with the new baby. Janet needed time to help little Jane adapt to the new situation. I had a day of shopping planned with Mother. While we were eating lunch, I couldn't help but notice, what an attractive woman my mother is, why today she just seemed to glow with happiness. I wish I had beautiful blue eyes like Mother. With that thought I realized my daddy had blue eyes also. How could my eyes be brown, almost black in fact?

"Mother, you look so happy today."

"Why, Suzanna, how does happy look, what do you mean?"

"Your eyes have a sparkle in them, and for the first time in my life, I realize I have a beautiful mother."

Mother's eyes were misty, when she replied, "My goodness, you embarrass me, but thank you for the sweet thought. You are right, I am very happy to be having this lovely day with my beautiful daughter. We haven't had a day like this in such a long, long time. I remember when you were small, when we shopped for your school clothes; we had this kind of day. I always looked forward to those school-shopping sprees. Even when you were a little girl, you would look at the price tags, before you tried on a garment. You acted as though we couldn't afford the best for you, do you remember that dear?"

"No, I don't remember per se, but I remember you telling me this before. Mother, why do I have brown eyes and you and Daddy have blue eyes? I noticed Mother becoming nervous with my question, it's beyond me why, but she had a trapped animal look in her eyes. All of a sudden, she hurriedly looked at her watch and said, "Oh, goodness, would you just look at the time, we should go now if we plan to get all our shopping done. Do you realize we have been sitting here over an hour? We still have to get something for the new baby, and the little girl, what is her name?" she asked gathering her bags.

"Her name is Jane Marie, and we still have plenty of time, if we wanted we could shop a couple of hours, and be home in plenty of time to fix supper." I got my shopping bag, and followed Mother out of the restaurant. It's times like this that have always puzzled me about my mother. Why would such a simple question, have such a drastic effect on Mother? The rest of the afternoon wasn't the same. We became strangers again. When we got home, Mother began to prepare super, suggesting that I should go up to my room, and wrap the gifts for Janet's children.

She doesn't want me to ask any more questions, so she's calling our time together to an end. I picked up my packages, and climbed the stairs to my room. I don't know why I even bother to ask questions, I never get any answers, all it does is cause more distance between me and

Mother. I thoroughly enjoyed wrapping every little gift. I could visualize Janet's excitement, as she opened the baby's gifts, and helped little Jane open hers. I'll be glad when Daddy gets home, and supper is over. I'm tired. The day has been a long one, and really stressful there, at the end.

Mother had been too generous, as always, I wouldn't need to go shopping anymore the rest of the summer. I know she insisted on me buying a short set for every day of the week. I didn't even count the sundresses. Enough underwear for three people, and nightshirts galore. Supper was quite and uneventful as usual, Daddy only grunting while Mother told him about our day of shopping. Later Daddy went into the study, to spend an hour or so with his Wall Street Journal. I helped Mother clear away the table in complete silence, and then excused myself to go get my bath and go to bed.

I was up early enough this morning to eat breakfast with Daddy, which was a shock to him, I think, from the comment he made. "Goodness, little girl, you must have another day of shopping planned, getting up this early.

"No, no more shopping for a while. I wanted to get an early start on the day, and I thought it would be kinda nice to have breakfast with you for a change. I hardly ever see you, and I never have a chance to talk with you."

"Well now, that's true," he answered, "Do you have a problem

Suzanna? You know I'm always here for you, at least I hope you do."

"No problem, just a friendly little chat is all I need, and yes I do know you will always be here for me."

Daddy didn't say another word, so I finished my toast and coffee, and excused myself, wishing him a good day, as I headed out the back door to the garage.

Janet and I sat at the kitchen table, while she fed Jane. Janet was looking so much better than a few days ago. "I hope I didn't come too early, I just thought there might be some cleaning I could do for you."

"Uh-uh, you are not too early, and I will gladly let you help with the house work."

"Just tell me where to start, in the meantime I'll get a load of clothes in the washer."

It was time to feed Jane her lunch by the time I got everything done. I fixed our lunch, while Janet took care of Joseph's needs. She finally got him and Jane down for a nap then we had time to visit without interruption.

"Gosh, Janet, having two kids is going to keep you busy full time. You couldn't have time for a job outside, even if you wanted to. Are you still thinking about having four children?"

"Not on your life, I was out of my mind to even think I wanted four kids. I do think Ricky is gonna straighten up his act thank goodness. You can't imagine how scary it is to think your marriage might fall apart, and you have two little ones to take care of all by yourself. There were so many times I thought I would lose my mind, while I was carrying Joseph."

"Yeah, I know how low you got Janet, thank goodness it's over. I worried about you for a change, and believe me it's just as difficult when the shoe is on the other foot. I really can't say which is the worst, to be the worrier, or to be the worried about. I guess you could say it's six of one or half a dozen of the other."

"I don't either, but I've never thought about it that way before, Suzanna. Now that's all water under the bridge, so let's move on to happier subjects. I want to ask you a personal question, and if you don't want to answer, just say so. I really meant it when I told you

I wouldn't meddle in your life anymore. I would just like to know, if Bill had asked you out the other day, what would have been your answer? I need this answer to satisfy my own curiosity, that's all."

"I can't say for sure, because at the time my emotions went haywire, just seeing him again."

"Yeah, I can imagine what a shock it would be, if it were me. What was your first thought though, seeing him in the gift shop, in the hospital?"

"To be honest, I was afraid he might be there to see his wife and baby. I had no way of knowing if he got married after I left or not. My heart sank, until I took a quick glance at his ring finger, to see if he wore a wedding band. I just hope he didn't notice me looking, but I'm not sure he didn't.

I doubt he will call me, if he wanted to go out with me again, I think he would have asked me there in person."

"Now just think about it, Suzanna, he was as tongue-tied as you were, so he probably didn't know how to ask you there in person. He might have thought about it, but was afraid you would say no, and he would rather hear that answer on the phone. I have a feeling he will call you, and I hope you will give him another chance. Bill is one of the nicest men I know, you could do a lot worse you know."

"Since I can't remember what happened on our last date, he might not be willing to give me another chance; this is what frightens me. How can I explain I don't remember our last date even if I tried, would he believe me? Do I tell him I tried to take my own life? That I had shock treatments to even have a resemblance of a normal life again? Can you tell me how to do this Janet?"

"I'm sorry, Suzanna, I can't tell you how. Maybe you could just go out with him, and hope something will bring your memory back, about that night. Maybe something he might say or do, would trigger your memory. You might never have to tell him those things, unless he tells you he loves you, and wants to marry you. You could stay just friends, who knows what might happen. One thing for sure, nothing will happen if you two don't ever get back together. Don't you agree?"

"I know you are probably right, but I'm not gonna get my hopes up that he will call me. It's been two days now since we saw each other, and he hasn't called yet."

"Don't give up whatever you do, Suzanna, You know he might be afraid you will reject him, and most men just can't handle rejection, women either for that matter."

"I have to go now, Janet, I need to help Mother with supper, and I feel the need for a long soak in the tub, before Daddy gets home."

"You don't know what a life saver you've been today, I'll never be able to repay you. Why don't you plan to have supper with us tomorrow night, and we could watch a movie or something."

"That sounds like a winner, I'll let you know later, after I make sure Mother isn't planning something. I doubt seriously she is, but just in case."

Janet walked me to the door, and waved as I drove away. I'm so lucky to have a friend like Janet. I don't know what I would do without her. She's the only person that I can talk to honestly about anything, and everything.

Chapter Thirty-Two

Janet decided to run her plan by Rick, while they were eating supper, since that was about the only time she could have his undivided attention. "Honey, do you think you might get Bill to come over here for super tomorrow night, or would that be in too short a time?"

"What have you conjured up now, for gosh sakes?"

"Now don't be that way, Ricky, after all you asked me to find out how Suzanna feels about Bill. Don't worry, I didn't mention anything you and I discussed. However I did ask her to eat supper with us tomorrow night. This is how they met the first time, so I figure it might work again. We won't tell either of them the other is invited, that way we won't have to worry that one of them won't show up. This way they won't have time to get nervous, about seeing each other again."

"Wait a minute, Janet, did you ask Suzanna if she would consider going out with Bill again, or did you just decide to get them back together regardless, for your own satisfaction maybe?"

"Ricky, you know I wouldn't do something like that, why I would be afraid Suzanna might never speak to me again. When she talks about Bill, anyone can see that she's in love with him, especially me being her best friend. You just don't get uptight about it I made sure she still has interest in him. She even told me she was afraid he might be married by now, especially seeing him in the hospital gift shop."

"Did you suggest to Suzanna that she is in love with Bill?"

"Uh-uh, I would never do that."

"Why didn't you, if you are so absolutely sure about it?"

"I halfway promised Suzanna that I would stay out of her love life. Ricky, you know how important it is to me for her to find happiness."

"I see honey, you don't think Suzanna will ever find happiness, without your help."

"Something like that, Janet answered with a little smile crossing her lips. Now will you please see if you can get Bill over here tomorrow night?"

"Okay, Janet, but if this blows up in your face, just don't go blaming me," Rick growled.

When Rick left the kitchen, he turned in the doorway, and observed how excited Janet was, he said, "Honey I do hope you know what you are doing, for your own sake, anyway."

"Oh, stop being a worry wart, go on and get your shower, and get ready to watch your ball game. Everything's gonna work out fine, you just wait and see."

Later after they were in bed, Janet just couldn't let things go.

"Ricky, please try your best to get Bill over tomorrow night."

"What would you have me do, Janet, twists his arm? He could have other plans you know."

"Yeah, but try to get him to change his plans. I know, tell him he just has to see your handsome little son. You can think of something to get him here, if you try hard enough."

"Don't you think if I get too anxious he's gonna wonder what's up. He hasn't been back to visit us, since they broke up. What if he ask if Suzanna's gonna be here, you don't expect me to lie do you?"

"Certainly not, if he ask you, you will have to tell him."

"I can't think of a reason he might think Suzanna would be here though."

"Janet, you are impossible. Just go to sleep, I've got to get some rest, it's getting late."

"Okay, dear," Janet answered in her sweetest voice. She doesn't think she will ever go to sleep. The excitement of the possibility of getting Bill, and Suzanna back together is overwhelming. She lay there planning the whole evening, in her mind, even right down to the conversation.

When I got to Janet's house, the next day, I couldn't believe how energetic she was, especially this soon after giving birth. She even polished the furniture, while I ran the vacuum. The phone rang, and she actually ran to answer it. I didn't know who it was, but it seemed they had good news, from Janet's expression. She decided the bathroom needed a good scrubbing. I had to insist she let me do it, because I thought it would be too strenuous for her right now. I wanted to ask why the house had to be spotless all of a sudden, but

I was afraid Janet might think I didn't want to help.

Janet bathed Joseph earlier than usual, she asked me to get Jane bathed and into her pajamas. When everything was done, Janet headed for the kitchen to start supper. I asked her why she was starting supper so early. She told me we were going to have a special supper, therefore it would take a little longer to fix. I told her she didn't have to fix anything special because of me. I knew she had to be tired, after all the housework we had done. It had only been a little over a week, since she had little Joseph, I told her she should slow down, if she didn't she wouldn't have the energy to care for the kids. Then she would get all grouchy and unhappy. She informed me to stop worrying about her, then she asked me how many kids I had had, in other words I didn't know what I was talking about. I told her if she insisted on being stubborn, to tell me how I could help her.

An hour later, the kitchen was full of mouth-watering aromas. The pot roast was about done, with the little new potatoes and baby carrots all around it. The beans and corn were done, and the rolls smelled wonderful in the oven. I made one of my scrumptious cheesecakes, with strawberry topping for desert. When we sat down to wait for Rick to get home, I made the remark that Janet would have enough leftovers for another meal. "It's not that much really, Suzanna, there are just more different things, than I usually fix, when you eat with us. You shouldn't complain. You have worked a week for one good meal."

"Janet, you are acting like I'm special company or something. I don't remember you ever using your tablecloth, and cloth napkins just for me. Is there something you forgot to tell me by chance?"

Janet just smiled and she said; "Only one little thing, I might have forgotten to tell you my friend. Why don't you go and freshen up before Ricky gets home? I promise when he gets here you will know what the surprise is."

I went back to the bathroom to brush through my hair, and maybe put on a little lip-stick. I couldn't imagine what the surprise could be. On my way back to the kitchen, I looked in on the baby. He is such a beautiful baby, and he's sleeping so peacefully, I envy him his innocence.

When I got back to the kitchen, I heard voices in the living room.

171

Who could that be, then I recognized Rick's voice. I walked toward the living room entrance, and peered around the door facing. My heart fluttered up into my throat. I should have known Janet would do something like this. Bill was the other male voice I had heard. Now I knew why everything had to be perfect today, I should have caught on before now, how could Janet do this? I took a deep breath, and entered the room. Bill had his back to the door, and didn't see me right away. "Hello Bill," I said, and he turned to face me. I could tell by his expression that he had been ambushed also. The meal was delicious, but at the beginning, Janet thought she had made a big mistake. The tension around the table was so thick; you could have cut it with a knife. No one said a word, while they were eating. Rick kept looking at Janet, with a frown on his brow, as if to say, this was your bright idea, now do something. Janet was lost for words, momentarily. Janet looked across the table at me and said, "I thought this would be a good surprise for you and Bill, but now I see I was wrong, and I want to apologize to both of you. I'm sorry, I keep telling myself I know what's best for everybody, and it's very clear to me now that I don't. Will you please forgive me, and I have to tell you, Ricky didn't have anything to do with this, so don't blame him. I don't know what I did wrong this time, it worked like a charm the first time I did it."

I smiled at Janet and replied, "You know I always forgive you, but I can't speak for Bill. He hasn't known you for years the way I have."

Janet's eyes met Bills, "will you please forgive me Bill, I didn't mean to make this visit stressful for you. I was just hoping you and Suzanna might get back together, at least for the summer. I guess I've earned the name busy-body, as far as you and Suzanna are concerned."

"I'll admit it has been a strange evening," said Bill, "but your intentions were good, so I'll have to forgive you too. It would be great to my way of thinking, if Suzanna and I could get back together."

Bill turned to me, "how would you like to see a show tonight with me, if we leave right away, we can get in on the first showing?"

When our eyes met, I felt my heart return to my throat.

172

"I would love to Bill, but Janet has planned to watch a movie here on TV tonight."

"Oh, okay, maybe another time. I didn't realize y'all already had plans for the evening." Rick all of a sudden jumped into the conversation. "That's okay, buddy, you and Suzanna are free to leave we understand. It won't offend us at all, will it Janet?"

"Oh, no," answered Janet, "I planned the movie only if nothing worked out for you two."

As Bill and I stood outside the front door, I asked Janet if she was sure that she and Rick didn't mind our leaving. "Of course I'm sure, after all what I planned to happen this evening, has already started," she laughed.

Janet and Rick walked back into the house, Rick's arm across her shoulder. Janet smugly asked, "Honey, what do you think of my idea now, I knew it would work."

"To tell you the truth, I was getting a little up-tight there for a while. I thought you had lost your lifetime friend, and helped me lose a good friend of mine in the bargain. Janet, that was a long shot, you do realize that don't you? You hafta promise me right now that you are through getting involved with Suzanna's love life. Is that clear?"

"Okay, I promise, don't run your blood pressure up, good grief Ricky, you'd think I robbed a bank or something."

They were watching the movie Janet had mentioned to Suzanna, but for the life of her, she couldn't follow the plot. She was too busy wondering what Bill and Suzanna were doing. She felt obligated to find Suzanna a husband, because she didn't think Suzanna was capable of surviving alone in the world. She could hardly wait for Suzanna to tell her all about their date. Then she remembered Suzanna had left her car here, so she would be coming back to pick it up. Maybe she could talk Suzanna into spending the night with them.

Chapter Thirty-Three

When Bill and I arrived at the picture show, we realized we both had seen the picture. Bill apologized for not finding out in advance, and asked me if I would like to do something else. I told him it didn't really matter, whatever he wanted to do would be fine. He suggested we could sit in the park and I could tell him all about school.

We walked along the path to the nearest bench. I couldn't help but notice how handsome he was, and so tall, I hadn't remembered him being that tall, but surely he hadn't grown since I last saw him. When we were seated, he said, "I don't know if we will want to sit here very long, I didn't realize how hard a cement bench could be, did you?"

"No, I can't say that I did. You know I've lived here almost all my life, and this is the first time I've ever sat in this park. I didn't even know the benches were made of cement, did you?"

"Uh-uh, I didn't, but actually I don't think I ever gave a thought to this park, before now.

I've walked through it lots of times, but I don't think I really saw it, if you know what I mean," he answered.

"It's so cool here, to be a summer night, and there is plenty of light. Of course this little town is crime free, so it is perfectly safe here. I don't remember there ever being anyone hurt here in my lifetime anyway, do you, Bill?"

"Oh no, it's perfectly safe to live here, I don't know anyone around home that even locks their doors."

We went on talking about our town, and I couldn't help but see how proud Bill seemed to live here. I had always felt kinda trapped here, after all there wasn't anything to do, but go to the picture show. I had secretly always dreamed of going far away from here, to live someday.

"Don't you wonder how it would be to live somewhere else, I asked?"

"I haven't ever thought about leaving here. I wouldn't know which way to go, north or south, if I left. Where would you like to live, Suzanna?"

"I've always thought it would be exciting to live in a big city, or in another country, even."

"I can tell you right now, I know I don't want to live in a big city. I've never even had a thought about leaving the United States, not for good anyway. It probably would be interesting to visit another country, but to live there, uh-uh, not me. I'm completely happy right where I'm at."

He stood up, and suggested we walk for a while. I didn't argue that, this bench was awfully hard, and they didn't even have a backrest on them. Whoever designed these benches didn't want anyone to stay too long in the park.

As we strolled along, he reached down and took my hand in his. The touch of his hand made the blood rush to my face, and I felt disoriented, a bit light headed in fact. I turned to face him, and casually took his other hand in mine. He misread my gesture and drew me into his arms. He bent and kissed me softly on my lips, I gently pushed him away. He stood there not knowing what to do or say. I knew then I owed him an explanation for my actions.

"Bill I'm sorry, but I need time to think about us. You don't know why I was in the hospital, and someday maybe I will tell you all about it, but I can't right now. I would like to be your friend again, if you feel the same way. You do mean a lot to me, please believe me, but we need to start over, and maybe things will be right this time."

"Okay, Suzanna, I can wait until you are ready. I'm sorry for my actions I guess I just read you wrong a while ago. You mean a lot to me too. I'm willing to start all over, and see what happens."

I looked at my watch, "Goodness, it's already midnight, and you have to work tomorrow. We should be getting back to Janet's."

"When can we get together again Suzanna? Do you need some time to think about it?"

"I tell you what, you give me a call at Janet's, say about next Monday evening."

We parked next to my car in the lot, and Bill got out and opened my door. When I got out of the car, I reached up on tiptoes, and kissed him on the cheek, and whispered, "Thanks Bill for being here for me."

"No problem," he said, with a break in his voice.

I looked up, and saw Janet hurrying down the walk. "Suzanna," she called.

"What in the world is wrong, Janet?"

"Nothing is wrong, I just wanted to tell you, you are welcome to spend the night with us," she said.

"It is a mite late to go home, and since you asked, yes I think I will stay over."

"Great, now let's go make a pot of coffee, and you can tell me all about tonight. Things must have went good, for you to be so late getting back."

"My goodness, Janet, where do you get all that energy? I'm ready to go to bed, tomorrow is another day, and we can talk then."

"I guess you are right, but I'm not a bit sleepy right now. Joseph will be getting me up for his next feeding in about two hours. I guess I do need the rest, goodnight Suzanna."

"Goodnight, Janet."

I lay on Janet's couch wide-awake. I couldn't believe how emotionally tiring the evening had been. In a way I wished the evening had never happened. If I had not seen Bill again, the turmoil in my heart would not have returned. I needed peace within, to reason things out where Bill was concerned. I have no control whatsoever of my emotions, when I am with him. I know in my heart that I can trust Bill, however I'm not sure I can trust myself, when we are together.

Morning finally came after a sleepless night. We are having coffee, and Janet is beside herself, wanting to know what happened with Bill last evening. "Now please tell me you and Bill are back together for good, Suzanna, I want to hear every little detail. Being out that late you must have smooched a little while."

"Janet, I'm sorry, but I'm afraid what I have to tell you is not necessarily what you want to hear. We had seen the picture that was showing, so we decided to walk in the park. We just talked, that's all."

"Mercy, I didn't lose all that sleep to hear the night was a bore. He did ask you for another date, didn't he? Tell me what really happened, Suzanna. You know you can trust me."

"If you just have to know what we talked about here goes, I explained to Bill that I needed time, and we should take it slowly. I think he understood what I was saying, because he agreed with me. I told him he could call me here Monday evening, I hope you don't mind. I'm just not ready to be interrogated by my parents just yet, anyway. You know as well as I do that's what will happen the minute they know I'm seeing Bill again."

"Yeah, I definitely know what you are saying about your folks. You know I don't care how often Bill calls you here. "Just tell me one thing, Suzanna, how long do you intend to string Bill along?"

I don't think it's a bit fair to him. I hope you know what a chance you are taking, because I don't think Bill will keep coming back, just to be hurt again. In fact he's much too intelligent for that kind of game."

"I'm not planning to hurt Bill. We just agreed to start all over again, as if we didn't know each other before, that's all. What is so unfair about that, for either of us?"

"Frankly, I don't believe it will work, Suzanna."

"Why, you told me you and Rick have started your marriage over. If you can make it work with your marriage, why can't we make it work with our friendship? A marriage is much more important than a friendship, don't you agree, Janet?"

"Of course, but it hasn't worked for us yet either. Look at it this way it's a lot easier to walk away from a friendship, than a marriage. The point I'm trying to make, Suzanna, is you better not think you can string Bill along indefinitely. You need to decide what you want from Bill. If it's not a relationship, then you need to let him get out of your life. You and I know that this friendship stuff you keep talking about, is just plain malarkey."

"I know what you are saying Janet, but it doesn't make me any more positive, about how I feel about Bill. I know you are usually right, but I want to get my teaching degree, before I commit myself to anything or anybody. I plan to tell Bill this, probably on our next date."

"Well, I should say so, Suzanna. He needs to know how long he would have to wait for you, that is if he's in love with you. I'm so glad you know what you want to do now though, and I think you will make a good teacher. Do you already know what grade you want to teach?"

"Yes, I want to teach kindergarten, or maybe first grade".

"I think they would be the age, to be most eager to learn, and the most fun to teach. I know I'm going back to school this fall, and if Bill does love me, he won't mind waiting. Of course he will have to volunteer to wait, I don't intend to ask that of him."

It's Monday evening, and I'm waiting for the call from Bill. I guess Janet sees how anxious I am, because she is being completely silent, which is hard for her to do. Finally the phone rings, and Janet waits for me to answer. When I pick up the receiver, Janet quietly leaves the room. "Hello."

"Hello, may I speak to Suzanna please?"

"Yes, Bill it's me."

"I didn't recognize your voice, I guess because I assumed Janet would answer. Have you had enough time to think about us? I would like to talk to you in person. I can never find anything to talk about on the telephone."

"I'm not overly fond of the telephone either. Sure we can talk in person. Can you come over, and pick me up, or should I meet you somewhere?"

"Sure I'll pick you up in about twenty minutes."

"Okay I'll see you then, goodbye."

I stood outside waiting for Bill. It wasn't near twenty minutes, when I saw him drive through the complex entrance. He stopped, and I didn't give him time to get out to open my door. I opened the door and slid inside.

"Where would you like to go?" he asked.

"You know I haven't given it a thought where we might go, have you?"

"All I know is we definitely don't want to sit in the park again, on those hard benches."

"Uh-uh, we don't." I laughed.

"Why don't we ride down to Indian Springs, we could walk the nature trail, and I'm almost sure the benches are made of wood," he said.

178

Indian Springs is a beautiful little state park. There's a stream running through the middle of the park. You can rent rowboats, and enjoy the exercise that way, or you can walk the well-lit trail beside the stream. If you want a little more excitement, a little corner of the park has a carnival atmosphere. There is a Ferris wheel and a skating rink, and a bowling alley. I have only been here once when I was a little girl, so this would be a real treat for me.

We parked and just sat there for a few minutes, taking in the beauty of nature, and the quietness not saying a word. Bill turned to me and asked what I would like to do first. "It's so beautiful here, why don't we take a walk first? I don't remember it being this nice when I came here before. I guess it could be because I was only ten years old at the time.

"Goodness, if I had known that, I would have brought you here before. I used to come here all the time, on dates and with the guys. I thought all the high school kids hung out here on weekends. Back then it was a really fun place to be, and not as expensive as a lot of other places. That was the main attraction for me, back in high school. I had a weekend job in a little gas station, and I had very little money to spend."

"I'm not sure where the kids in high school with me hung out. I didn't date anyone in school with me, and I didn't hang out with the crowd, so to speak. I guess you could call me a bore, back then, not very many of the guys ever asked me out. The ones that did were mostly clowns, and I wouldn't have been seen with them."

"I can't imagine that, Suzanna, I liked you from the minute we met, and you are definitely not a bore. You are an interesting person. I enjoy being with you. You are the first girl I've ever dated that I can be myself, and comfortable with. Believe me, if I had that last date we had to do over, I would not lose control, the way I did that night. You will never know how sorry I am for letting things get out of hand. I promise you it will never happen again."

"Wait! Wait! Bill, I need to tell you something, before we continue this conversation. The reason I was in the hospital was because I tried to take my own life. I held my wrists out before him, to show him the scars. I still don't know why I did it, but I hadn't been well in quite a while. I was seeing a psychiatrist, and he wouldn't let me leave the hospital without some kind of treatment.

They tried several kinds of medications, none worked. Then Dr. Shannon thought maybe shock therapy might work. I didn't know how drastic that would be, so I agreed to it, and signed the papers. When I was through with the shock, it left most everything that had happened to me before, just one big blank. Bill I have no memory of our former friendship. I'm not sure I'm ready to face what you were talking about happened on our last date. I am sure though that I will completely understand, if you don't want to see me anymore, after tonight."

He put his hands on my shoulders then quickly took them away again. He had such a look of pure pain on his face. "I'm so very, very sorry, Suzanna, Why didn't Rick tell me what was going on. He told me you had been in the hospital, but he didn't tell me what was wrong. I would have contacted you when you got back home, but after our last date, I wasn't sure you would ever want to see me again. I'm so sorry I wasn't there for you, if only I had known. Are you alright now?"

"If you are asking me if I will ever try to destroy myself again, I won't, that's a promise. I'm alright on that one count, but I'm not sure I will ever be completely alright."

"I think I understand what you are saying, the most important thing is you will never try to kill yourself again. One question, how do you know for sure you won't, if you don't know why you did it the first time?"

"I know for sure, because I've lost two dear friends since you and I were together. This gave me an understanding of how much it hurts the ones who are left behind in this world. I hope I've changed for the better, since you and I first knew each other. I also need to tell you that I plan to go back to college and get my teaching degree, before I make any changes in my life. I need to prove to myself that I can complete one thing in my life. You don't owe me anything. No matter what happened the last night we were together, my trying to take my life wasn't your fault. I should have told you up front I was under a doctor's care. You had a right to know I was a troubled person, emotionally and mentally. I'm sorry I wasn't honest with you, then all this might not have happened at all."

"It wasn't all your fault either, Suzanna. You told me from the beginning that you were not ready for a relationship. I'm proud of you for wanting to finish your education. I feel like I'm just drifting through life myself right now. I don't have any long- term plans for my future; I haven't even given it a thought the last couple of years. I've been helping my folks make ends meet, and that's the extent of my life, since we quit seeing each other."

"Bill you need to think about going to college, you should save your money for a couple of years. Then go to school as far as that will take you, go every other quarter, and work every other quarter, if you have to. You can find a way if you set your mind to it, I know."

"Maybe someday I can, but right now I'm helping my folks get more secure for their future. I'm helping them buy the property where they live, that will take at least another year, then maybe I can think about my future."

"Oh, that's a wonderful thing you are doing. I know your folks must be very proud of you. You must love them very much."

"I surely do, don't you love your folks that much, Suzanna. I'm sure if they needed your help, you would be there for them."

We went out in the rowboats, and we even rode the Ferris wheel. We laughed so much my side was sore. When we returned to the car, I told Bill that this had been the best night of my life. I told him I had enjoyed every minute, and that I hoped we could come back again. Then I happened to think that he might not be planning to ask me out again. What I had just said might make him feel obligated to do so. I turned toward him, to try to explain myself if I could.

But when our eyes met, I knew I didn't need to explain anything. Bill put his arm around my shoulder and pulled me close. I lay my head against his chest, and we sat quietly for several minutes. Then he said, "You are the only girl I've ever been this close to, and I hope you will go out with me until you have to go back to school. I can't promise what the future may hold for us, but I hope you will always at least be my friend. Maybe we will be only friends, but I want you to be a part of my life forever, Suzanna."

I looked up into his eyes, and I could see moisture collecting. I sat back away from him and said, "Bill I feel the same way about you.

I've never felt this way about anyone else. I will be honored to go out with you the rest of the summer. When I go back to school, if you want me to I will write to you. That is if you promise to write back."

"I would like that a lot, and I will answer every one of your letters. Don't you have a phone in your dorm?"

"No, the school is quite strict. They will let you use the office phone once in a while, but no longer than three minutes."

"You are gonna have to tell me more about this school, while we are together this summer. Right now I need to get you home."

Bill walked me to the door, when we got home. He took my hands in his and said, "Goodnight Suzanna, it was a fun night, I'll call you later." Then he turned and walked to his car.

"Goodnight Bill," I whispered to myself. While I was preparing for bed, I realized I had peace within, like I had never felt before. I lay in bed, and tried to visualize the rest of the summer. Will I be strong enough to go back and finish my education, or will I fall in love with Bill? He won't be free to marry me for another couple of years, so I will have time to get my degree. I had planned never to come back to this little town to live, but Bill loves it here.

Will the voice ever go away? I suppose only time will tell.

*